The Wolf's Secret

WILD MAGIC: LUNAR LEGENDS
BOOK ONE

STEPHANIE MIRRO

Linley Press

Also by Stephanie Mirro

THE LAST PHOENIX

Wings of Fire

Wings of Death

Wings of Winter

Wings of Magic

Wings of Life

Wings of Deceit

Wings of Mercy

IMMORTAL RELICS

Curse of the Vampire

Fury of the Gods

Revenge of the Witch

Rise of the Demons

WILD MAGIC: LUNAR LEGENDS

The Witch's Lie

The Wolf's Secret

The Pack's Fate

WILD MAGIC: SIREN'S SECRET

Siren's Tale

Siren's Blood

Siren's Gift

Siren's Legacy

COLLECTIONS

Rejected Mates: A Paranormal Romance and Urban Fantasy Collection

The Outsiders: An Hourlings Anthology

You can also **download my FREE short story Oneira the Dream Maker,** a Silver Honorable Mention recipient from the Writers of the Future contest.

I love to get to know my readers. Find me on Facebook, Instagram, or Twitter **@stephaniemirro**.

Visit stephaniemirro.com for more information on each of my books.

Part One

CHAPTER 1
Rose

Under the full moon's pale light, I ran like the devil was chasing me...

Because he was.

Not the actual Devil, as in the King of the Underworld himself, thankfully, but a man who deserved an eternity in Hell just as much.

Branches snagged on my shirt and hair and tore through my skin. My lungs ached with each gasping breath, and my legs threatened to buckle beneath me. I pushed past the pain, refusing to give up. I couldn't.

He'd kill me if I did.

I couldn't believe I'd been so stupid, so naive. I couldn't understand how I hadn't seen the signs right from the start, the dangerous glint in his dark eyes. Looking back, they were so obvious.

Even if I hadn't discovered his secret, he never would have let me go, not with his demented fantasy that we were destined to be together. That we were *mates*.

As I ran through the dark woods, I almost snorted at the

ridiculous thought. Wolves and other shapeshifters had mates, not witches. We weren't some lesser animal like them, functioning off animalistic needs and instincts.

Witches were chosen by the moon goddess herself, gifted with magic to fulfill her sacred tasks.

Shouts pierced through the trees behind me, startling me back into focus. I forced my legs to pump harder, ignoring the burn in my calves and thighs. Being on the track team through high school and college had come in handy, though I'd never thought I'd use my love of running to escape a nightmare.

Unfortunately, I had never trained in the middle of the forest at night. I tripped over a hidden root and crashed onto my hands and knees. My breath whooshed out, and wet dirt soaked through my jeans. My wrist twisted and cracked under my weight.

A stabbing pain ricocheted up my arm, and I held my wrist to my chest, biting down on my lip to keep from crying out. Moisture formed in my eyes, and I wanted nothing more than to lie down and rest, to let the moon's glow heal me.

Except, I couldn't stop—their shouts were getting closer.

Get up, Rose, I urged my tired limbs to obey. On shaking legs, I stood and threw myself forward. My mouth had never been so dry; my lips cracked and raw and stinging in the wind.

It wasn't like I planned on running tonight. I would've wanted to be more prepared and have a go-bag packed at the very least. I hadn't had a chance to grab my wallet and money or decent running shoes. Not even to bring Mouse, my only real friend in those last few days.

I huffed out a laugh. Yes, my friend list had narrowed down to one tiny furred creature who loved to sit on my shoulder in the evening and curl up on my bed during the day.

Somehow we understood each other, even though he never spoke back. I missed those little squeaks already, and I vowed to rescue him once I was back on my feet again. Hell, the whole coven needed saving.

If only Josef hadn't walked in when he did.

Images of the horrors I'd discovered returned, raising goosebumps across my skin. Images of women he'd claimed left his retreat voluntarily. I found them half-dead and strapped to operating tables, attached tubes siphoning their magic from their unconscious figures.

And when he found me there...

Shudders racked my body and threatened to spill me onto the ground again. I shoved the memories away. I'd have to deal with those feelings later.

How the others hadn't seen through his façade too was beyond me. Sure, I'd thought he was charming and handsome at the beginning of the retreat, just like everyone else had. But it had only taken a few months for me to see through to his true colors.

Well, that wasn't quite true. It had taken seeing it for myself to truly believe he was capable of such atrocities. If I hadn't been attacked and forced to run for my life, I could have proven it to the others once and for all.

An owl hooted somewhere amidst the branches overhead, and the far-distant calls of hunting wolves drifted over the canopies. I prayed that they were too far away to pick up our scent because if they found witches trespassing in their territory, we'd all be dead.

Not that I cared so much about Josef's life, but *I* certainly wanted to live, and most of the others had been my friends once. They'd been deceived, just as I had. Someday, I'd help them see the truth, and they'd come to their senses.

Holding onto that hope might be the only thing keeping me going.

My wrist ached with every jostling step, and I clutched it tighter to my chest. I also hoped that the next town wasn't much farther because I wouldn't last, not at this speed. Not even with my running background.

The only saving grace was the time of year. Fleeing through these woods in the depths of winter would have been a death sentence. Instead, I only had to deal with swarms of insects that stuck to my sweat-soaked skin, and the muggy air didn't help that situation.

A branch snapped behind me, much closer than I would have expected. Fresh tears formed in my eyes. I couldn't let him catch me. Not now, not after what I saw and what he would do to me next.

There would be no more second chances.

Why, oh why, had I returned?

Heavy footsteps and huffing breath closed in, heard even over the wind rushing past my ears. If I didn't do something quick, I would need to make a stand, and there was no way I'd win in my current state.

A glance up reminded me that it was a full moon close to the summer solstice, which was a blessing and a curse for someone like me. My magic would be at its highest level tonight. Lunar magic wasn't as common as the others, and it was sometimes feared, or coveted as Josef had done.

A cloudless full moon night also made hiding next to impossible.

For most people, anyway.

I reached outward with my mind, drawing the shadows to me. They came in wisps and tendrils, curling around me eagerly, ready to do my bidding. When I gathered what I hoped would be enough, I prayed to the moon goddess to guide my spell.

Skidding to a stop, I whirled around and threw my arms up, grimacing as the sudden move tweaked my injured wrist. The shadows I'd gathered sped forward, engulfing the man who ran into sight. Our gazes met for the briefest of moments, and Josef's dark eyes sparkled with malicious desire.

"Don't run from me, Rose," he warned in a low voice. "You being mine is inevit—"

My spell swallowed him whole, and the smothering blackness

muffled his angry shouts. I spun on my heel and ran, choking back a sob. That was way too close.

Other coven members' urgent voices carried through the woods as they caught up to him and tried to break through my spell. It would take them a while since my magic was so potent during a full moon. Had it been just one of them, I might have stood a chance at fighting back.

For the umpteenth time, I almost wished I didn't have this magic either. He wouldn't have noticed me then.

Only...

Who would he have obsessed over instead? And what would he have done to her?

Howls sang in the distance, closer than they'd been before. Goosebumps broke out across my skin despite the dripping sweat, and pinpricks crept across my scalp.

Had they heard all the shouting? Were they on their way?

A full moon meant mating night for the wolves. With any luck, those animals would be too busy rutting in the dirt to notice us or give us much thought.

If not, then as evil as it sounded, I hoped they found the coven first. I didn't wish harm on any of the others, but they'd listened to his lies.

A tear slipped down my cheek only to be whisked away by the wind. My shoes pounded against the forest floor as I tired, losing the energy to move more stealthily. My pulse thudded in my ears and drowned out most of the forest sounds.

The howls continued, and soon, so did fearful shouts from the coven. I glanced over my shoulder. Above the trees, sparks of light shot into the sky, accompanied by pops and crackles. The witches had blended their magic to break my spell binding Josef.

They were going to draw the wolves' attention for sure, as if they didn't know how dangerous it was to be in these woods.

Didn't they value their lives?

Sharp jabs dug into my arms and legs, and I cried out from the unexpected pain. Not watching where I was going, I'd plowed straight into a bramble thicket.

Cursing under my breath, I extracted myself from the thorny branches, tugging at my jacket sleeve as it caught. Wolves called to each other, closer. Panic seized my lungs tight, and I yanked harder at the caught sleeve.

The fabric ripped, and I stumbled away from the claw-like bushes. I sucked in a gasping breath and dropped to the ground, crawling beneath the thick brambles. I hoped that they—witches *or* wolves—would think I'd stopped at the thicket and gone the other way.

Thorns shredded my clothes and skin as I crawled. I bit back another sob as warmth trickled down my face and across my back until I heaved myself through the last of the brambles and stood on shaking legs.

The bushes behind me burst into flames, and I gasped. Two witches stood on the thicket's other side. Their familiar features wavered in the fire's heat, but the hatred in Beverly's expression was undeniable.

I spun and ran, praying the bushes would burn slowly. Wolves barked only a short distance away, and I banked to the left, away from the sound.

Except my body wasn't ready for that quick of a move. I tripped over my own foot and flew forward. Expecting to hit the ground again, I windmilled my arms as I kept flying.

When I finally smacked into the ground, my breath left my body in a violent rush. I bounced head over heels down a steep hill, rocks and sticks gouging into my skin and dirt filling my mouth and eyes.

The hill evened out, and I thumped to a stop, collapsing onto my side. Spitting out dirt and leaves and gasping for breath, I rolled onto my back. Growls and barks announced the wolves' arrival at the top of the hill, as did the witches' subsequent shouting and screams.

As I panted, I blinked up at the moon. The bright light blurred in my vision. A concussion, possibly. It was hard to tell—everything hurt. My chest rose and fell as I sucked in deep breaths, and the small charm I kept on a chain slid toward my neck.

Reaching up with a trembling arm, I clasped the sapphire charm and squeezed my eyes shut. Tears slid down my face, hitting the leaves beneath my head with small splashes.

If only I hadn't left home. If only I'd listened to my parents' warning. It was almost like my mom and dad knew Josef had lied about everything, and now I would never have the chance to tell them they were right.

My mom had given me this charm before I left home a year ago, making me recite the spell until I had it memorized. I'd told her she was being ridiculous, that nothing would ever be bad enough to warrant using such a spell.

Then I left in a huff like a total idiot.

None of us knew it would be the last time we saw each other. No one expected them to lose control of their car, taking them from me forever.

Leaves rustled farther up the hill. Someone was sure to come down the slope at any moment. Someone, or some *wolf*.

Either way, I would be dead if I didn't make a move.

Summoning the last bit of energy I had, I opened my eyes and focused on the moon, drawing on its energy for strength. I rolled onto my side and put my foot beneath me to stand. Stabbing pain ricocheted up my calf, and I collapsed back onto the ground, my ankle throbbing.

Shit.

I was out of options. I clutched the charm again, my heart thudding hard against my ribs.

If I did this, there was no going back. It was against the rules, against the covens' law. This spell was unthinkable for my kind...

Forbidden.

But as the crunching leaves and snapping twigs veered closer to the ravine's edge, my time had run out.

Beneath my breath, I chanted the spell my mother had taught me and prayed to Luna that it would work in time. It had to. Changing my nature, the very essence of who I was, was the only way to survive.

I had to become a monster.

CHAPTER 2

Liam - Twelve hours earlier

Sunlight filtered in through the bedroom window and across my eyes. Cursing myself for not drawing the curtains last night, I threw my arm over my face, not quite ready to face the day. The full moon had come too fast this month.

The slight scent of stale beer mixed with honeysuckle reached my nose, and I released a quiet groan when I remembered I wasn't alone. I glanced over at my bedmate.

Amanda's blonde hair, which was just long enough to reach her shoulders when she stood, fanned out over the pillow beside me. Her tanned shoulders and bare back weren't covered by the sheet, and I knew the rest of her was fully naked beneath the thin fabric.

She hadn't done anything wrong to deserve my groan. The opposite, in fact. She was exactly what I needed last night. Almost exactly, anyway, but she'd satisfied my needs and I hers. In the past, that was as far as it would ever get with Amanda.

She might wish that my wolf and I would claim her beneath a full moon like the one tonight, but she had never been what I wanted in a mate. No one in this pack was my fated mate or intrigued me enough as a potential partner, but I wouldn't have the luxury of waiting much longer.

A strong alpha needed a mate, fated or not.

Someone rapped lightly on the door. It cracked open, and Caleb stuck his head in. His deep brown eyes glanced between Amanda and me before rolling skyward.

My beta didn't understand what I saw in Amanda, and honestly, sometimes I didn't either. She was crass, brutally direct, and could drink most wolves under the table without a hint of a hangover the next morning.

Out of the pack's view, she had a soft, kind side that made her blue eyes sparkle, especially when it came to the cubs. She would make for a fearsome mother.

And behind closed doors, she was an animal. The sex was great, and my wolf enjoyed the frequent release until we found a proper mate. Even though he and I had agreed Amanda wasn't proper for *us*, she might be our only option.

Caleb tilted his head for me to follow and disappeared. I dropped my feet to the floor silently, but Amanda stirred.

"Mm, good morning." Her voice was still sleepy, giving it a breathy, sultry edge. As she rolled over, the top sheet caught beneath her leg, revealing her naked breasts and stomach.

It was a shame she wasn't my fated mate. Those full, perky breasts made just about every man's mouth water, and her tanned, toned figure came from years of running through the woods. She was as much of a skilled hunter as any of the others—more so than most, a fact she loved to rub in their faces.

But as alpha, I needed more from my partner than good looks and hunting skills. I needed an equal, someone whose leadership the pack respected. Simply put, that someone wasn't Amanda.

I stood and crossed to the dresser. "Caleb needs me."

"He can wait," she purred, sitting up so that she was visible in the mirror over the dresser.

Catching me look her way, she held my gaze as she ran a hand over her breast, pinching her budding nipple slightly. She slid her hand lower, over her flat stomach, until it disappeared under the sheet.

Her soft moan nearly did me in, but as the pack's leader, I had duties to attend to, and right now I didn't mean my dick.

Are you sure? my wolf asked, his excitement rising.

If I let him have his way, we'd never get any work done.

"You know your way out," I said and shut the bathroom door behind me.

Something thudded against the door, likely a pillow. I smirked and started the shower. She'd get over it. If not, I'd remind her of her place. She was one of my advisors and a friend with benefits. Nothing more for now, and she knew it.

After a quick wash and fresh clothes, I combed my hair. The blond strands were dark from the water and dampened my shirt. I hadn't bothered to cut it over the last year, not since I took over as alpha.

I met my blue-eyed gaze in the mirror, hating the tortured look that always stared back. Everyone knew I would be the next alpha after my father, but knowing didn't make the job any easier.

If I hadn't stepped in when I did, he would have destroyed the pack, and ripped every wolf to pieces in his grief-fueled rage. As his son and the next strongest wolf, putting him down had been my responsibility.

My father had understood, but his dying breath still haunted my dreams.

Shaking off the unwelcome memory, I left the bathroom and found the bedroom empty. Relief lowered my shoulders. As expected, Amanda knew her place, even if she thrived on pushing boundaries.

Waiting in the hall outside my room, Caleb leaned against the wall with his arms crossed.

My beta was my opposite in many ways, with short, curly black hair and brown eyes that almost matched his hair depending on the light. He and his twin sister Mallory shared the same light brown skin, born from a white mother and a Black father.

Because I was an only child, Caleb and Mallory had been as close to me as siblings. Their mom and dad were like second parents, even more so over the past year. They were currently on a much-needed and well-deserved summer-long European vacation.

Caleb's gregarious personality was well-received by our pack, and his witty commentary made it easier for me to be the hardass. Good cop, bad cop. That had been us since we were little more than cubs.

Today, his demeanor was more reserved, and his unique peppermint and pine scent was thick in the air. Neither of which were good signs.

"There's been another kill," he said, uncrossing his arms as he followed me down the stairs to my cabin's main level.

I should have known better than to bother with clothes.

"Where? When?" I asked, already dreading the answers.

This would be the third unsanctioned hunt on our lands in as many months. Our pack controlled almost fifty miles of the Shenandoah woods south of Front Royal, but rival packs had been pressing in recently, claiming the loss of their lands due to human construction.

Like any other species, shapeshifters could live wherever we pleased, but wolves preferred the less populated mountainous regions. My pack had lived in this village for generations, and with proper care and attention, we would for generations to come.

After ducking through the opened door leading into the kitchen, I nodded to Cecilia who bustled about the stove cooking breakfast. The grey-haired woman had been with our pack since my grandfather was a cub, yet she had outlived every other wolf from that time.

Some of the pack teased that she would outlive us all. As a rare red wolf, she was a gifted seer, and the exceptional accuracy of her visions only added credence to the jokes.

Except the prophecy she saw for me when I took over as alpha was anything but a joke. It could mean the utter destruction of everything I held dear.

"They hunted early this morning, near Dark Hollow Falls," Caleb said.

When Cecilia turned to look at me, he snuck around her side and snagged a piece of bacon. Lightning fast, her wooden spoon cracked down on his hand, and he yelped and dropped the bacon back onto the plate.

She shook the spoon at him and scowled. "No food until it's on the table."

I smiled. Despite her advanced age and stooped frame, no one messed with Cecilia. She was a force to be reckoned with.

Holding his hand to his chest as if injured, Caleb offered her his infamous sad puppy eyes. "Can you blame me? Your cooking is the envy of every pack in the National Park. Probably the entire east coast."

As she muttered and returned to the stove, I bent to kiss the top of her head, at least a foot below my chin. We weren't related by blood, but she was like a grandmother to me and had lived in my home for years before my parents' passing, cooking every day without complaint.

I'd make sure she was happy and wanted for nothing until her final day.

She shuffled toward the cabinets. "Sit. I'll get you both plates."

"We'll eat when we get back," I promised and nodded Caleb out the kitchen's back door.

Facing the forest, we stripped and let our wolves take over, our bones snapping and reforming in a matter of seconds while fur sprouted across our skin. Caleb's wolf was nearly as large as mine, but his coat was a more typical dark grey for a beta while mine was pure black.

The majority of wolves had shades of grey, brown, and tan fur.

The darker the color, the more likely the wolf would be strong enough to become an alpha.

White and silver didn't equate to weakness, however. Although not as uncommon as black, white wolves were thought to be blessed by Luna herself and often became alphas' mates or their closest advisors.

Red was the rarest of all, designating some sort of psychic ability like Cecilia. Typically, they drifted between packs and didn't settle in one spot for too long. Cecilia was an anomaly staying with us for so long, though she visited other communities from time to time.

Caleb and I raced into the surrounding woods. Our pack's main village wasn't too far from the human town of Syria, Virginia, which was where we went for shipments and supplies we couldn't make ourselves.

For the most part, we were self-sufficient and lived off the human grid. Solar panels provided enough electricity for our basic needs and technology, and we distilled moonshine with our bountiful potato and corn crops.

Technically, we didn't have a license to distill alcohol, but considering some of our best customers worked in state government, we weren't too worried about getting shut down. Still, a handful of wolves accepted jobs as park rangers as a source of backup income and for tax and paperwork purposes.

Dark Hollow Falls was about eight miles away as the crow flies. Normal wolves would need an hour or two to get there, but we weren't normal wolves.

Within a half hour, we'd picked up the rival pack's scent and tracked it to the deer's remains. The bones were mostly picked clean from wolves and scavengers. Before shifting back to human form, my wolf and I sniffed the area.

A dozen wolves had been through here, and only two were from my pack. Their scents were the most recent since they'd discovered the unsanctioned kill, but I recognized the other wolves' scents just as easily. This wasn't their first infringement.

My wolf and I growled, and our hackles raised. This was a blatant challenge to our lands, and I would not let it go unpunished. I couldn't—failure to do so would appear weak, an alpha no longer worthy of his pack.

Caleb and I shifted back to two legs, a change that ceased to hurt decades ago. Only the earliest weeks of shifting caused pain, but those days had been excruciating.

"I know you're willing to let accidents go," Caleb gestured to what was left of the deer, "but this is no accident. Three's not a coincidence, and they sent at least ten wolves in this time."

I rubbed my chin, belatedly realizing I'd forgotten to shave before I showered. Amanda's naked body and roving hand had been more of a distraction than I cared to admit.

"Then it's time we hit back," I said. "I want maps of their territory and schematics of their homes. I also want routines and schedules. We don't make a move until we can be certain that any cubs will be out of harm's way."

Caleb nodded but made no attempt to follow through with my orders. He had something else on his mind.

I raised an eyebrow. "Go ahead."

My beta cleared his throat as he met my gaze and held it. Whatever he was about to say, I wasn't going to like it.

"You need to claim a mate tonight," he said, cutting straight to the point. "The prophecy said—"

I held up a hand. "I know what the prophecy said, but my fated mate is not in our pack. You know that as well as I do."

Caleb let out his breath and ran a hand through his dark hair. "It's always possible you'll feel something new on the run tonight. You and I both know that fighting the Massanutten Howlers will cost more than we can afford. If this goes much further, lives will be at stake. *Wolves'* lives."

He was right, of course. He usually was, which was one of the reasons he was such a nuisance.

The Howlers had pressed their luck by hunting on our lands, but they also outnumbered my wolves, the Skyline Pack.

"I'm open to whomever Luna chooses for me, but I don't believe picking a mate just to do it is the answer," I said at last.

Cecilia's visions had proven true time and time again, even if we misinterpreted them. There was no reason to start doubting them now.

"Maybe not, but it can't hurt, right?" he asked.

For once, I disagreed with him. Choosing the wrong partner could hurt quite a bit.

Especially if my fated mate ever showed up.

CHAPTER 3

Liam

The campfire's roaring flames cast shadows over the surrounding area, dancing and tangling with the trees and edges of darkness like old friends. Hefty, worn logs circled the fire, providing plenty of seating for those pack members not joining the mating run until the rest of us returned.

Tonight, the summer moon was full and bright, not a cloud in the sky to block her radiance. Whether they were participating or not, most of my pack gathered around this fire, coming from small communities all across our territory. They would cheer on the wolves running and celebrate any unions when we returned.

Our wolves were restless within us, visible as fidgeting movements and darting gazes. Laughter rang out around the camp as contagious excitement grew.

Every month, our unmated wolves of eligible age ran together beneath the full moon, surrendering control to our wolves as we sought and selected mates. Luna played a significant role in that task, guiding us toward our fated mates whenever possible.

Some were too eager to wait for a fated mate, which was understandable and hadn't resulted in any issues in the past. There was always a chance the non-fated union would turn out poorly, but it was also possible the fated bond broke once a wolf chose another mate. Only Luna knew for sure.

Not all wolves found their fated mates in their lifetime, but the goddess did her best to create happy unions. Only once in our long history had a fated mating gone wrong, centuries ago, when one wolf rejected his chosen mate.

The rejection was the primary cause for our split from the witches and the root of our deep hatred toward each other. Betrayal and lies had caused too many deaths, marking it as one of our history's darkest times.

The story had become something of an old wives' tale, but Cecilia swore that it was true and should never be forgotten. I believed her, and with any luck, it would never happen again.

My gaze wandered over the less familiar faces who'd traveled in, but no spark indicated my fated mate was among them. Yet again. I hadn't expected her to suddenly appear, but my level of hope could be a fickle fuck.

No one was surprised I hadn't claimed a partner yet; mates worthy of an alpha were few and far between. But tonight, I might have to do what was best for the pack even if it meant giving up on ever finding my fated mate.

Having a strong partner by my side would strengthen my pack, especially once we produced a few cubs. With encroaching rivals, we needed to be as strong as possible, and soon.

The thick, mouthwatering scent of honeysuckle closed in. Amanda's arm brushed against mine, and my wolf made a sound of appreciation. She was my best option out of those gathered.

I ground my teeth together as the pack elders addressed the crowd, blessing the wolves about to run beneath Luna's bright gaze. I hated that my options for a mate came down to settling. A wolf should never have to settle.

The elders finished their speeches, and the crowd cheered as pack members stripped their clothes in a rush. Some of the younger wolves competed with each other for the fastest to bare it all.

I followed their lead and tossed my clothes into a pile. Growing up in a wolf pack, nudity was a daily occurrence and far from taboo. It was almost as normal as breathing, and stripping before shifting saved a fair bit of money in the wardrobe department.

Tonight's summer heat and campfire provided more than enough warmth for bare skin in our two-legged forms. But even in the dead of winter, the shift would turn into a competition as the frosty air nipped at our shivering limbs.

A warm hand ran up my thigh, edging inward.

"Do not disrespect me in front of the pack," I growled low so only Amanda could hear. "Or ever."

She dropped her hand and rolled her eyes, a bold move that made me wonder if I'd been too lenient with her over the years. She met my gaze straight on. "After tonight, it won't be seen as disrespectful. You'll be mine."

With that taunt, my wolf took over. He leaped forward in our consciousness, ripping through my skin and fracturing my bones with resounding cracks. Pitch-black fur sprouted across my limbs, covering my body in a heartbeat.

Pack members around the camp surrendered to their wolves willingly, and sometimes unexpectedly, as their wolves followed their alpha. Shades of brown, grey, and hints of red or silver gathered together, nuzzling and playfully swatting and nipping at one another.

My wolf and I raised our black snout to the sky and howled, a long, lonely sound that the others quickly took up and drowned out. Their excitement reverberated through the air, as contagious as their laughter had been. I wished I could share in their carefree revelry.

We raced for the woods, leading the charge. Winding through trees and trails we'd known since cubhood, we ran. Other wolves caught up, their fur blurring by as we took turns passing each other, delighting in the group activity. Here and there, wolves would break off in their own game of chase as Luna urged them into a union.

Soon it will be our turn, my wolf said with undeniable eagerness and a hint of wistfulness. He wanted a fated mate as much as I did, but he was less willing to wait.

A smaller grey wolf from an outlying community made her way into our periphery, panting hard as she struggled to keep pace with us. As alpha, we were the biggest, strongest, and fastest of our pack. We had to be to keep every member safe.

The wolf caught our eye, interested and looking for reciprocation, but there was no spark. No recognition within my wolf or me that this meeting was fated. We peeled off to the left, leaving her behind.

Two more females approached in similar ways, and both times we left them disappointed. Neither of them had been our mate, not a single spark or twinge of excitement.

None of them were Amanda either, my wolf noted, his tone irritated.

I laughed in our joined thoughts. *Still holding out hope that Luna will change her mind on that one?*

His growl just made my mental smile bigger.

A sudden scent caught on the wind, and our nostrils flared —danger.

Without slowing, we howled out a warning and called for a hunt through our shared pack consciousness. It wasn't a telepathic ability; more like connected emotions. Younger wolves would return to the fire, and my hunters would join me.

We chased after the scent, and a familiar brown wolf edged closer, her gaze taunting me even now. As much as my wolf wanted me to forget the fantasy of a Luna-blessed union, this was not the time to be thinking of claiming anyone. Not with the potential danger on the wind.

The scent grew stronger, and recognition sparked a new kind of eagerness within me.

Witches, my wolf and I thought in unison, surprise tinting both our tones.

What were witches doing on pack lands?

Deep growls erupted around us as others recognized the hated scent. By the strength of the smell, there had to be at least a dozen, an entire coven. Their hubris knew no bounds, and we would be glad to remind them of their place.

My wolf and I slowed as a new scent blended with the breeze. Something up ahead was burning. Our pack slunk forward, ready to attack our mortal enemies.

We wouldn't kill them unless necessary; we weren't complete savages. But we'd enjoy frightening them.

As we cleared a thick copse of trees, a smoldering bramble bush barred our way forward. Crackling flames devoured the dry, blackened branches, which crumbled to the forest floor, and ash covered the grass and foliage around the bushes.

My hunters spread out, sniffing the area to determine which way the witches had gone. Caleb barked farther along the bush, and my wolf and I headed toward him. The witches' stench grew stronger as we approached.

Tilting our head and sniffing the air, we stopped as another new scent drifted toward us. Our ears perked up, and we trotted toward the spot Caleb had found. A strip of cloth hung from a thorny branch.

An unfamiliar sensation rose within us, along with unmistakable arousal. Whoever this scent belonged to, it attracted us like nothing ever had. We sniffed the cloth, relishing in the zaps of electricity that zinged through our body with each inhale.

Our mate? my wolf asked.

It had to be. Desire clouded our senses, nearly drowning out everything else.

Caleb barked again, drawing our attention to a narrow path

between the brambles. We needed to deal with the witches' threat before we could track down the scent's owner.

After casting a final longing glance at the fabric, we led the way through the path, our hunters right on our heels. The witches' scent built until we spotted them beside a steep ravine.

We lifted our snout and howled, calling for the attack. Like legends born from nightmares, we tore from the trees and surrounded them. Snarling and baring our teeth, saliva dripped from our mouths.

Their cowardly eyes widened, reeking of terror as they huddled closer together.

Growling in warning, we lowered our head and eyed the man we assumed was their leader. He pushed the others behind him and faced us fearlessly as he chanted. Emerald magic swirled thickly around him.

We lunged, and our teeth snagged on a fluttering skirt as it disappeared, along with the rest of the coven.

That was when scents hit us hard—the owner of the ripped fabric and the metallic rust of blood. She was nearby and injured. If those witches had harmed her, we would rip out their hearts and swallow them whole.

From the bottom of the ravine, a bloodcurdling scream pierced the air, raising the fur along our back. Icicles of fear stabbed through our heart.

We dove for the steep side, leaves and branches crunching under paw as we slipped and slid our way down. Through our shared consciousness, our hunters questioned our blind leap and urged us to wait.

Except the call of fate was stronger, and I'd waited long enough to answer.

CHAPTER 4

Rose

My mother had taught me the spell that would save my life, but she'd failed to warn me about the pain. The excruciating, soul-shattering torture as I changed into something I wasn't supposed to be.

Screaming in agony as my body ripped itself apart atom by atom, I writhed among the leaves and fallen branches. My arms and ears lengthened, and new teeth sprouted from my gums within my elongated snout.

As my bones cracked and stretched, reforming into a shape other than human, a blinding light filled my vision.

Suddenly, it was over, the pain only an echo of a memory. I sagged against the ground and panted, too exhausted to lift my head.

Bushes rustled and a massive wolf stepped forward. His coat was as black as midnight and shining like freshly scribbled ink. His eyes were such a perfect blue, like a clear summer sky.

He laid his ears flat against his lowered head, though I somehow knew he wasn't threatening me. It was the opposite—he seemed cautious yet curious.

Whimpering, I tried to raise my head a fraction of an inch

before it became too heavy to hold. An odd feeling came from my lower back as though I was waving my arm. White fur flashed across my periphery, and I wanted to laugh. I had a tail.

The only way to survive this night was to hide in plain sight, and the spell had worked.

I'd become a monster—a disgusting wolf.

Well, I looked, smelled, and acted like a wolf. I hadn't turned into an actual shapeshifter with an animal spirit residing inside me, thank the goddess, but no one would know that little fact except me.

My mother hadn't said why she'd chosen this form out of all the supernatural creatures when she created the charm, but I assumed it was because of the retreat's location. Josef's family estate in Shenandoah Valley bordered known packlands.

Regardless of her reasoning, my mom had given me the key to my survival.

The black wolf stepped closer, his tail wagging behind him, though his eyes still regarded me with caution. He lowered his head to mine and sniffed, our noses touching briefly.

Sparks zapped across my body as if handling a live wire. Heat surged through every part of me and pooled low in my belly.

When he drew away, the sensations faded, leaving me breathless as I stared up at him.

What in the world had just happened?

Several more wolves dashed into view. Their lips drew back from their teeth in threatening snarls, and they snapped powerful jaws in my direction.

Fear flooded through me, and I lowered my head, flattening my ears. If any of them sensed the truth about me, then I was as good as dead. There would be no more second chances.

The black wolf was bigger than any of the others, and he barked back, growling as he stepped over me.

Protecting me.

Confusion invaded the others' gazes, mirroring my bewilderment. I had no idea why the wolf above me was defending me, but finding out—or communicating at all—was impossible in this form. I took a deep breath, steeling myself for the pain, and willed my body to return to my human shape.

The forbidden spell that camouflaged the essence of who I was could only be cast when the moon was at its fullest. It would last a month, until the next full moon, and allow me to change forms at will until then.

Although, I wouldn't need to shift again after this encounter. All I needed right now was to get away from Josef.

Fingers crossed the wolves took care of him, I thought.

As my body contorted and shifted, fur and claws retracting, I clenched my jaw. The incredible pain was nowhere near as bad as the first time, but I was glad that it was the last time I would have to experience the unnatural torture.

Cold, wet earth squished beneath my fingers as I pushed myself upright, and my arms shook with the effort.

The big wolf above me sensed my movements and leaped gracefully away. He faced me, and his wolfish gaze raked over my body.

Belatedly, I realized that I was naked. Head to toe, buck naked, my clothes shredded around me thanks to the quick shapeshifting.

Good one, Rose.

It took all my willpower not to cover myself with my hands. Wolves were perfectly comfortable with nudity, and they wouldn't believe my lie if I tried to hide. Instead, I tilted my head forward, letting my long black hair cover what it could naturally.

I didn't trust myself to stand just yet, but some of my strength had returned, and the throb in my wrist and ankle had dulled.

Witches healed faster than humans, but wolves surpassed witches. Maybe the spell had given me a boost for extra fast healing. One minor blessing on this hateful night.

"I'd li—" My voice was hoarse and cracked, and I cleared my

throat before trying again. "I'd like to request safe passage through your lands."

The black wolf's gaze never left mine as he shifted to his human shape. Like me, he was as naked as the day he arrived in this world, and I'd be lying if I said I didn't stare.

Might have drooled a bit, too.

This man was as massive as his wolf and built into pure perfection. Muscles that must have been chiseled from stone rippled beneath his broad shoulders and chest, his skin tanned to a golden bronze.

Dark ink spread along his arms and over his shoulders. Judging by the pattern, I'd bet the tattoo continued down his back.

His abs were a well-defined eight-pack, and a deeply indented V led straight down to...

I tore my gaze away, and heat rose in my cheeks.

Holy shit.

His sizable genetics did not stop with his muscles.

I forced myself to look up at his face. He didn't appear to be much older than me, possibly in his late twenties or early thirties. Blond hair fell around his shoulders, and a light scruff hugged his chin but did little to hide his strong jawline.

His nose was classically straight and drew my eye up his sharp cheekbones to his eyes. And, oh, wow. What unbelievable eyes. Even in his human form, they were so blue, so intense.

I swallowed hard, my mouth watering.

What was I doing again?

"Safe passage to where?" His deep, gravelly voice rumbled through me, striking every nerve, igniting within me until I was about to combust.

Oh, dear goddess.

I licked my lips, acutely aware of his gaze tracking the movement. "Anywhere but here."

He narrowed his eyes. "Why?"

"I'm being hunted by witches," I managed to stammer out.

This man was affecting me in a way I'd never experienced. I kind of liked it, but I kind of hated it at the same time. I mean, he was a wolf, for Luna's sake. Gross.

The man's gaze flicked to the side, and a moment later, several wolves tore off into the trees. He looked at me again with those beautiful blue eyes, and my breath caught in my throat.

I swear he could see right down into my soul.

"Who's your alpha?" The volume of his voice dropped with his next question like he was mystified. That made two of us. "Who are you?"

"I'm..." I couldn't tell him who I was. If he looked up my name, he would know my secret and immediately kill me for deceiving him. I scrunched my eyebrows together. "I'm not sure. Everything's fuzzy past this evening."

Technically, none of what I said was untrue. If I needed to change my identity to hide from the coven, I wasn't sure who I would be.

Plus, I'd hit my head hard in that fall down the hill, a fact my body enjoyed reminding me of just then. Nausea twisted in my stomach.

A light brown wolf padded closer and shifted into human form. Like the man, the change took only a few seconds, except this wolf was a woman.

Make that a drop-dead gorgeous woman. Blonde hair fell in choppy waves to her shoulders, and she glared at me with deep blue eyes that sparkled with danger.

There wasn't an ounce of fat on her body aside from her voluptuous curves. She was any man's wet dream come to life.

She stepped up to the man's side and put her hand on his arm.

Instantly, the hairs on my nape raised. I wanted to slap her for even touching him as if I were jealous of a man I didn't even know. Not just a man—a wolf. I swallowed hard.

What the hell was wrong with me?

The man glanced at her hand then her face, the lines of his jaw moving as he clenched his teeth.

She removed her hand but stayed close. "This can't be a coincidence."

My heart leaped to my throat. A coincidence? With what? What mess had I run into?

"She doesn't smell like them." His deep voice rolled through me again, making my body respond in the best and worst way possible.

"Like who?" I asked, trying to ignore the traitorous sensations.

Blondie glared at me. "He wasn't talking to you."

A deep growl came from the man's throat, and the woman took a step back, frowning.

I took a deep breath and sucked in my pride. Time to go full birthday suit. Urging my body to obey, I tucked my legs beneath me and stood.

My injured ankle rebelled, and my vision swam as a woozy, dizzy feeling took over. I nearly toppled over sideways, but strong arms wrapped around me, keeping me upright.

"Thank you. I hurt my ankle in the fall..." my voice trailed off as I tilted my head toward the incredibly handsome man who had caught me.

Dark brown eyes twinkled down at me, amusement spreading across the man's light brown face. Adorable freckles sprinkled across his cheeks and nose. His curly black hair was cut short, and his body was just as muscular as the other man's.

Wolves definitely stayed fit, which might be their only redeeming quality.

"Caleb," the other man growled.

A shiver ran down my spine, but it wasn't from fear. Not even close.

I needed to get out of here.

"She's barely standing, man," Caleb said, his arms loosening around me but not letting go. "Look at her. She needs help."

Glancing down at my body, I immediately regretted it. Numerous cuts marked my skin, and streaks of blood and dirt covered just about every inch. My ankle and wrist were bruised and swollen, and leaves and berries stuck out of my black hair, all the way to my waist.

I looked like a flea-bitten mongrel.

"Absolutely not." Blondie crossed her arms, smushing her breasts into her chest. "She's one of them. There's no other explanation."

I had no idea who they were talking about, but my gut told me it wasn't the witches. Guessing she'd just bark at me again, I bit back my question. Besides, I needed to save the little energy I had for getting away.

"Maybe she's got a concussion," Caleb suggested, adjusting his grip on my arms.

His move brought my head closer to him, and his wolfish heat drew me in. Without thinking about what I was doing, I rested my head against his bare chest, and my eyes drifted closed.

"Sanctuary," I murmured. "Please."

Caleb's body stiffened as I relaxed against him, but a breath later he was ripped away from me. Strong arms scooped me off my feet before I collapsed, and I looked up beneath heavy eyelids.

Intense blue eyes stared down at me.

This man, this massive wolf who made my body react in odd ways, carried me through the trees as if I weighed little more than a feather. His body heat, a characteristic of the wolves I found delightful right now, enveloped me like a warm blanket.

I breathed in his scent, a warm, rich smell of fir that reminded me of Christmas. Happy memories from long ago bubbled up, of wintry mornings and ringing laughter. Of hot cocoa by a roaring fire.

For the first time in months, I felt safe.

I let out a contented sigh...

...and passed out.

CHAPTER 5
Liam

I ordered my hunters to keep up the search for the witches, but I had little hope of finding them within our woods. Their leader had been prepared for a quick escape.

One of my fastest hunters had returned to the village for a Jeep, driving it to the Dark Hollow Falls so we could bring the mysterious woman who'd fallen asleep in my arms with us. Although, I was reluctant to let go of her, even for the short drive back.

By the time we turned onto the winding dirt road leading into the pack's village, the campfire crowd had dispersed. I breathed a sigh of relief as we parked, not quite ready to share the sleeping woman with anyone else.

As gently as I could, I picked her up from the Jeep's backseat. She barely stirred except to curl against me again.

She was a conundrum. Everything about her exterior screamed fragility—lily white skin that was unblemished from the sun, hair so black it glinted blue under the moonlight, and the most alluring pink lips I'd ever laid eyes on. Her voice had been rich, calling to me like the full moon's song.

Only her grey irises had betrayed her steely interior. Even now as I carried her up the porch steps and into my home, strength and power exuded from her figure, tantalizing my senses and driving my wolf mad. It didn't help that she was still naked, and her body fit perfectly against mine.

Unable to resist another glance, I dragged my gaze across her breasts and nipples, hardened from the fresh mountain air. As I imagined what those rosy buds must taste like, my cock stiffened, and my grip around her tightened.

A soft moan escaped her lips, and I nearly tripped on a step leading up to my second floor. Taking a deep, steadying breath, I continued up the stairs and into my bedroom, the only room on this level.

I don't care what pack she belongs to, my wolf growled. *She's a mate worthy of any alpha.*

It was my turn to growl. No one but me would touch this woman, and if what my wolf and I felt was real, that would hold true for the rest of our lives.

My mate.

And here I thought I would never find a worthy mate, and I would have to settle for less. Luna worked in mysterious, sometimes frustrating, ways.

Our *mate,* my wolf corrected.

I laid the woman down on my bed and took a brief moment to look her over for any significant injuries. That was the reason I told myself, anyway.

Streaks of mud and blood covered her skin and hid most of the bruises and scrapes. She'd need a shower soon to make sure no infections took root, as unlikely as that was for wolves. A small tattoo on her inner ankle peeked out, covered by her other calf.

Gently, I moved her leg a few inches to see the design, unable to stop myself from stroking her silken skin with my thumb. The tattoo was a rose with deep red petals the color of blood and a thorny stem. An interesting choice, one she probably made on a whim in college.

Many wolves spent a few years away from their pack after

reaching adulthood. Some attended university while others traveled and explored the world. Those who mated right away were usually content to remain in pack life.

She looked young, only a few years into adulthood but old enough to have finished college already. If she'd gotten that tattoo in college, then she was likely unmated, a thought that triggered a happy rumble through my chest.

When I finally covered her with a blanket, I regretted the decision, wanting to memorize every inch of her while I could. Shame flushed through me almost immediately.

Yes, she was a vision to behold, but she had been through something traumatic tonight. The last thing she needed was waking up to my possessive, lust-filled gaze as I drank in her curves.

That's exactly what she needs, my wolf argued. *We need to claim her, now.*

A thrill of excitement and barely restrained desire surged through me, and I grew hard so fast I had to turn away. Claiming her would come but only when it was a conscious and mutual decision.

All in good time, I said, chuckling at his answering grumble.

My wolf's spirit had been with our pack for several generations and sometimes forgot he wasn't all wolf. Wolves' spirits stayed within a pack for as long as possible, choosing new hosts once their previous two-legged bodies closed their eyes for the last time. Transition ceremonies occurred shortly after a cub's birth.

I'd learned to ignore or control most of my wolf's base instincts over the years. So, as much as I wanted to claim this woman, I worried about Cecilia's prophecy and what it might mean for my pack.

While the prophecy had only mentioned a fated mate, I couldn't confirm anything about this woman while she slept. She was undeniably a worthy mate, but fated? Unease prickled across my scalp.

Only time would tell.

A creak on the floorboard alerted me to another's presence a moment before the scent of honeysuckle trickled in. I lifted my gaze to find Amanda staring at me with narrowed eyes, her hand gripping the door frame tight.

"Really? You put her in your bed?" She stepped farther into the room and anger radiated off her naked skin. "At least chain the bitch."

Before I knew what I was doing, I gripped Amanda by the throat, pressing her hard against the wall. Her deep blue eyes flew open as she gasped. Deep growls filled the room, and it took me a moment to realize it came from me. From my wolf.

If you don't calm the fuck down, we're going to have serious problems here, I snapped, hauling him back where he belonged.

Amanda's gaze smoldered, and the scent of her arousal drifted beneath my nose. Her hand moved between my legs, stroking my stiffened length. But my lingering erection wasn't from Amanda's presence.

Instead of turning me on as she always had in the past, I wanted to rip her head off for what she'd said about the sleeping woman. I settled for letting Amanda go and backing out of her grip.

Disappointment and confusion flashed across her face as she dropped her hand.

"Uh, what'd I miss?" Caleb stood in the doorway, his eyebrows raised as he looked between Amanda and me.

"Nothing." I glanced at the woman on my bed, hoping she hadn't witnessed or heard any of that. Amanda wasn't a threat. Far from it.

The woman's chest rose and fell with the deep breaths of sleep.

Amanda rubbed at the red marks on her neck. "I *advised* him to chain her up."

When I shot her a warning look, she dropped her gaze to the floor, finally remembering her place. She might have been one of my closest advisors and a long-time friend, but I was still her alpha first and foremost.

"If she's from the Massanutten Howlers pack, then she's a spy or just really stupid," she continued. "Either way, we can't let her escape."

Caleb nodded as he entered the room. Unlike Amanda, he'd taken the time to throw on some sweatpants and a t-shirt. "She's right, and if she is from their pack, we can use her for information. Or maybe as leverage."

I crossed my arms. "Nothing will be decided until we know for sure whether she's a Howler. But I agree that she needs to be bound." My gaze flicked to Amanda. "Bring me the chains."

Her upper lip curled into a snarl, but she obeyed and left the room, stomping her way down the stairs

Caleb grinned. "Ooh, boy. You're in for some trouble with that one."

"She'll fall in line or face the consequences," I said flatly.

"I've seen those on the receiving end of Amanda's wrath. I do *not* envy you, brother." He leaned against the door frame and glanced at the sleeping woman. "Talk to me."

I let out a breath and rubbed the back of my neck. As my beta and closest friend, there was little I could hide from him. "We're fairly certain she's our fated mate."

His mouth dropped open, then he laughed so hard, I had to shush him, worried he'd wake her.

"Oh, sorry, man," he said, wiping tears from his eyes as he chortled. "But that's fucked up. The night you're about to settle, this one practically falls into your lap." He kissed his fingers and tossed them away in a chef's kiss. "Luna's fucking with you real good. Fated? For real?"

That was a hell of an understatement. "It gets worse. I was going to claim Amanda tonight, and she knows it."

This time, Caleb's guffaws made me grin until metal clanking together reached our ears. We sobered as Amanda strode in carrying the heavy, wolf-resistant chains we used to secure out-of-control wolves. Now, they'd secure our prisoner.

A low growl rumbled in my chest. This woman wasn't a prisoner any more than Amanda was, but I had to put my pack's safety first. If only for perception's sake.

"Caleb, you're on the first watch. Call for me the moment she wakes."

I left them there to bind the woman's arms and legs to the wall hooks. Every bedroom in our village had them installed, just in case an incident involving an out-of-control wolf arose. Events like that were rare but being prepared was one of the first steps I'd taken as the new alpha.

No one should suffer the way our pack did before I was forced to take my father down.

Outside my house, the cooler night air and Luna's bright light washed over me. I needed to run out the adrenaline and desire that still pumped through my veins, so I let my wolf take over.

On four paws we ran through the woods, the trees and bushes blurring by as we pushed ourselves to the limits. When our muscles finally grew tired hours later, we trotted our way back to the place near the falls where we'd found the unknown wolf.

We sniffed the area, trying to determine anything else about where this mysterious woman came from or from which pack. Her clothes littered the grassy area in shredded scraps, but there was no other scent on them but hers. She was like a ghost.

No, she was much more than that.

She was a walking, talking dream come true.

Even in her wolf form, she was perfect. She'd had a coat of pure white beneath the blood and grime. White was an uncommon color, thought to be a blessing from Luna herself. Her eyes had been gold and almost glowed against the forest's darkness behind her.

After an intense search, my wolf and I had no more idea of who she was or where she'd come from than when we first saw her.

We were about to return home when a flash of blue reflecting the moonlight caught our eye. Nestled within the grass close to where she'd lain was a necklace with a dangling sapphire-hued stone.

We lowered our head and picked it up in our mouth, only to yelp and drop it. Our tongue and skin burned. The necklace was made of silver.

How had she worn such a piece?

There was no denying it was hers; her scent was all over it. We glanced at her destroyed clothing. She'd worn jeans and a jacket, which meant she could have had the necklace in a pocket. We would have to leave it here for now, until we came back with a backpack.

But why would a wolf keep a silver necklace with her?

We raised our gaze to the full moon, tilting our head to the side with curiosity.

Why did Luna bring us together tonight of all nights, the anniversary of the night I received the prophecy?

CHAPTER 6

Josef

J osef paced the length of the windowless room, grinding his teeth together hard enough to hurt. Good. He welcomed the pain.

He had been so close, so *fucking* close. If those pesky wolves hadn't interfered, he would have had her.

Now, the only other person with whom he shared his secret—besides the three witches with him now—had vanished into the night.

Glancing at the women strapped to their beds, he smiled, and his shoulders dipped with relief. Tubes attached to their unconscious bodies siphoned the magic from each, storing their supernatural essences in protective containers.

Thick stone walls and extra insulation in the ceiling sound-proofed the entire basement beneath the Weber estate. He'd converted the space into a lab, where it had taken years to perfect his invention. Years of trial and error and ridicule from his peers.

He wasn't the monster Rose thought he was, had screamed at him before she fled into the night. It wasn't as though he was killing anyone. Besides that first one, anyway, but he had fixed his mistake.

41

Not like anyone cared about Constance anyway.

Megan moaned, and he moved quickly to the woman's side. Taking her hand in his, he stroked the length of her arm, careful not to jostle the tubing. "Hush now, Megan. You're safe with me."

His voice soothed her subconscious, and she settled into a deep sleep once again.

See? Proof that he wasn't a monster.

No, he was freeing these women. After he removed their magic, they would be as special as a human, which is to say not at all. As a further mercy, they wouldn't remember a thing about their past lives or his secret.

Soon, it wouldn't matter who knew. He would share his brilliance with the world, and he would be unstoppable. Soon...

...but not yet.

Their pathetic magic was hardly worth having. If you thought about it, he was doing them a favor. No one deserved to be bullied the way he had been.

It wasn't his fault he'd been born controlling the earth element, considered the lowliest of them all. His parents had been fools to marry for love rather than think of what was best for their children.

Had they chosen proper partners, he might have been lucky enough to control air or fire. Regardless, his magic was still stronger than those he siphoned from now, even though their elements ranked as more powerful.

The only one whose magic he truly wanted was Rose's. His mouth watered at the image of her. She had no idea just how beautiful she was. Not just with her looks, but her unbelievable magic. So rare, so powerful.

She had no idea how truly special she was.

If she hadn't followed him before he was ready and ruined his plans, he could have shown her. Then she'd escaped from his lab and ran into the wolves' territory, forcing his hand. The coven had made far too much noise in their attempt to catch her.

Because it had to happen tonight, the night of a full moon when those rabid dogs were chasing each other down and fucking like animals in the dirt.

Josef clenched his fist and slammed it into the nearest wall. Sharp pain roared through his knuckles and up his arm. He winced and shook out his bloody hand.

"See what you made me do, Rose?" he muttered as he strode to his workbench.

He snatched up the healing salve and rubbed it over his broken skin. Immediately, the magic took effect, and he sighed in relief.

She'd been surprised to find out the other witches believed him over her. After everything he had done for the coven, who would ever believe her lies? Believe that he was evil?

The timer dinged, alerting him that the containers holding the witches' magic were full. Excitement prickled through him, and he spun on his heel.

Humming an upbeat tune he'd learned from his days on the stage, he replaced the containers. The magic trickled into the new canisters much slower than it had before. He grinned.

Not much longer now.

After adding the necessary ingredients to the siphoned magic, he removed the finished potions from the condenser and set the containers in their place. The machine whirred and beeped as it started up the process once again.

Soon, the magical gas would turn into a liquid, ready for him to consume.

"Bottoms up," he said cheerily before draining both finished potions.

The red liquid bubbled and burned as it went down, and he grimaced. He'd have to work on the flavor and temperature in the future.

As the new magic took root within him, blending with the magic he'd already consumed, he raised a hand. Flames danced across his palm, stretching higher and higher until they licked and scorched the ceiling.

Closing his fist to extinguish the fire, Josef smiled.

Not much longer at all.

/ *CHAPTER 7*

Rose

Letting out a soft groan, I rolled over onto my side. Every muscle and bone was sore, and every inch of my body felt battered and bruised. A fluffy pillow with a familiar fir scent cushioned my head, and I smiled.

Wait...

My eyes flew open. I sat up with a start, and the sheet slipped down to my waist. Thick metal manacles secured my wrists, and the attached chains were fastened to hooks behind the bed. I glanced around the room as I tried to remember where the hell I was and how I'd gotten here.

My gaze landed on a handsome young man with black hair and light brown skin lounging in a chair by the door. He looked vaguely familiar.

One leg was crossed over his other knee, and he held a book open on his lap. His dark brown eyes focused on mine, and I gasped as memories of the night before returned in a rush.

I also remembered I was still naked.

Gripping the sheet to my chest as warmth crept up my neck and cheeks, I gave him my best glare.

My fierce look only resulted in him chuckling and turning a page in his book. "Nothing I haven't seen before, love."

"I'm not your love," I snapped. "Where am I? Who are you? Why am I chained?"

He closed his book and raised an eyebrow. "Manners ain't your thing, huh?"

Oh, hell no. This guy knew nothing about me. "When I wake up in a stranger's bed *naked*, my manners are the least of my concerns, *sir*."

His teeth flashed as he grinned. "My boy's gotten himself into some trouble."

Dread trickled into my belly. If there was another reason I was naked in this bed, they'd find themselves on a fast track to meeting Luna herself. A one-way track.

My grip tightened on the sheets. "What do you mean?"

His eyes widened as he must have understood where my thoughts went. He dropped his foot to the floor and leaned forward, his hands raised. "Oh, goddess, no. Not that. You're safe here, I promise. He'd rip apart anyone if they laid a hand on you. And I mean anyone."

I drew my eyebrows together. "Who would?"

There was no time to answer before the door slammed open hard enough to rattle the windows, and a beast strode in.

Not an actual beast. Not even a wolf.

It was *him*.

The man from last night, the one who made my insides turn squishy.

His blond hair just barely brushed his shoulders, and dark stubble covered a strong chin. His blue eyes fixed on me as a predator did with its prey. So intense, it sent shivers down my back and heat straight to my core.

Sadly, he had clothes on today, but his black t-shirt stretched tight over his muscles, straining against the fabric. His tattoos were more visible in the daylight, some sort of scrollwork design in black ink that wound around his sculpted biceps and forearms.

Jeans hugged his thighs like they were painted on. They weren't a slim fit either, but nothing could contain this man's strength.

This beast's power.

He was raw, unrestrained lust incarnate.

And right now, his lust was focused on *me.*

Closing my eyes, I clenched my thighs together as an intense, sudden need rocketed through me. I had no idea why my body was reacting so strongly to him, but I wanted to throw up.

Well, my body didn't want to, but my mind sure did.

He was a wolf, for Luna's sake. A fucking animal. Witches and wolves were mortal enemies and had been for centuries. There was no way I could be attracted to one.

I must have hit my head harder than I thought. That was the only explanation. Or maybe it was because I was a lunar witch, and I had some weird connection to wolf shifters.

Except, my body only seemed to go crazy around one wolf in particular.

The door clicked shut, and I cracked an eye open. The other man had left, leaving me alone with the one who looked like sex on a stick.

While I was naked.

In bed.

Maybe even *his* bed, if that mouthwatering smell of Christmas trees drifting off the sheets belonged to him. Fingers crossed it was the detergent.

As the silence stretched on between us, he just stood there, staring at me with narrowed eyes, as if peering into my soul. I gulped, and his intense gaze moved to my throat.

"Who are you?" he asked.

His voice sank into me, deep and penetrating. Claiming me.

That tantalizing thought rippled through me like fire and ice, licking its way down my skin until it reached the apex of my thighs.

Somehow restraining another traitorous shudder of desire, I arched an eyebrow. "You first."

"Liam McDonnell, alpha of the Skyline Pack."

Liam.

Something inside my heart and mind flickered with his name like it was familiar. Which made no sense considering we'd only just met.

He crossed his arms, his biceps bulging. How the sleeves of his t-shirt stayed intact had to involve magic. "Why were you on our lands?"

"I was being chased, hunted." Goosebumps rose along my arms as I remembered my desperate flight into the woods. The coven had gotten so close. I might not have survived if I hadn't done what I did.

Or if the wolves hadn't believed my lie.

"Hunted by those witches." His tone didn't indicate a question, so I didn't respond. "Why?"

Time to think like a wolf. Ugh. My nostrils flared like I smelled something gross when really I was just thinking about something gross, like being a wolf. "Why do witches do anything? They're monsters."

His gaze traveled across my arms and chest, lingering on the swell of my breasts visible above the sheet. "Did they hurt you?"

Heat flushed across my chest in the wake of his gaze, but I raised my chin. "They tried."

A low rumble emitted from his throat, and his blue eyes darkened with promised violence. "Unfortunately, before we found you, they got away using a teleportation spell. They're no longer on our lands."

Damn. I knew death by wolf was too much to ask for. A man like Josef Weber wouldn't let himself get caught that easily.

"What's your name?" Liam asked.

Time to see if those high school plays taught me anything about acting. I took a deep breath. "I'm not sure."

Once again his gaze darkened, though this time, the danger was directed at me. He stood calmly, but incredible power and the potential for lethal violence radiated off him.

I knew without a shadow of a doubt that he could kill me with his bare hands before I took my next breath.

"You're making this situation very difficult." His voice held a hint of warning.

So nice of him to have some empathy for my amnesiac plight through the woods. Fake amnesia, but whatever.

I resisted the urge to gulp again. "Try putting yourself in my shoes. You wake up one day to find yourself held captive, with no idea who you are anymore. You escape, only to be hunted down by your captors, only to be captured and chained up once again."

None of it was a lie, either. Josef had tricked me, used me until I had no one left to turn to, no one I could trust. Thinking I was doing the right thing by staying as long as I did, I'd become someone I didn't recognize anymore.

I could never go back to who I once was—Rosalind Drake was as good as dead. I just had no idea who I would be going forward.

Liam grabbed the back of a chair and brought it closer to the bed before sitting. He leaned forward, elbows on his knees, and clasped his hands together. His blue eyes traced the outline of my face and neck, following the curves of my figure beneath the sheet, all the way to my feet.

Such a simple look, but my body responded like the traitor it'd turned out to be, warming beneath his gaze. I wanted his tongue to follow those same lines.

Wait, what?

I blinked.

What the hell was wrong with me?

His nostrils flared, and the corner of his mouth quirked up in a delightfully sinful smirk. He dragged his gaze back up to mine. "Well, for now, let's call you Rose."

My heart thundered, and I could scarcely breathe. He had figured out who I was.

But how?

More importantly, why wasn't I dead yet?

"The tattoo on your ankle," he explained, nodding at my covered foot. "It's a rose. Seems appropriate until your memories return."

My racing pulse drummed in my ears, but I managed to force a nod. Talk about a close call. "Okay."

Rescuing me with a well-timed distraction, the door opened and the man from earlier walked in. Delicious smells wafted down from a tray he carried.

My mouth watered and my stomach grumbled in response.

The man grinned and approached the other side of the bed. He set the tray beside me, revealing a plate full of eggs, bacon, and perfectly browned toast smothered in butter. "Do I have good timing or what?"

Liam leaned back in the chair, an amused look on his face. "Caleb, this is Rose. A pseudonym until she remembers her real one."

Goddess, this charade was hard enough to keep up as it was. Now they were using my actual name. As soon as I could, I would leave this nightmare behind me.

Moisture formed in my eyes, threatening to spill over. I hated crying in front of people, but the worst part was, the emotion wasn't from everything I'd endured over the last few months or the things Josef had done.

No, this grief came from somewhere unexpected and confused the hell out of me. I was reluctant to leave this unfamiliar and dangerous place, to leave Liam.

And now I needed to get my head checked out.

Electricity streaked up my arm as he took my hand, stroking the back of it with his thumb. "Did I upset you?"

Upset me? Ha! This man did everything *except* upset me, which was a huge part of the problem. He was being kind and gentle and completely caught me off guard.

I snatched my hand away, wincing as the manacle rubbed against my wrist's raw skin. "No, but I would love to eat without these damn chains. And some clothes would be nice."

Liam grabbed my arm despite my yelped protest and inspected my red, chafed skin. His accompanying growls raised goosebumps across my skin and hardened my nipples.

No clue whether that last reaction was from the room's sudden chill or my body's rising heat.

Liam's gaze snapped to Caleb. "Did you secure these?"

"Er, no." Caleb backed away, holding his hands up in a show of surrender. "Want me to get her? Yeah, I'll go get her."

He turned for the door and smacked straight into someone walking in. They both yelled in surprise and stumbled back.

I almost laughed. Wolves prided themselves on their heightened senses, yet these two had collided in a comically human fashion.

The blonde woman I'd seen earlier—now dressed in leggings and a tank top, which didn't do much to hide her toned body—punched Caleb in the arm, and not playfully either. "What the fuck, Cal?"

As her gaze moved to Liam and his hands still on my arm, Caleb skipped out of the room with a gleeful wave over the woman's shoulder.

Liam stood so fast, the chair toppled over and banged against the floor behind him. His upper lip curled with a vicious snarl. "Amanda, give me the key. Now."

Although his anger wasn't directed at me, I swallowed hard. Lethal ferocity curled around him like an expensive cologne, creating all sorts of conflicting feelings in my body and thoughts.

To her credit, Amanda didn't cower or hesitate. She dropped the key into his outstretched palm. "You-know-who's here. He's at the gate."

Despite his muscular frame and tangible anger, Liam's touch was almost delicate as he turned my hand to unlock the manacles. He leaned in close and inhaled as he removed them.

Is he...smelling me?

Gross. I probably smelled like stale blood, caked-on mud, and goddess knows what else considering my hasty escape through the woods. Body odor for days.

I held a tender wrist to my chest, rubbing the skin gently. "Thank you. Clothes?"

Amanda crossed her arms and let out a huff. "He said he can't stay long. You're going to miss his check-in."

Liam strode to the dresser and pulled a shirt from a drawer. Tossing it to me, he headed for the door. His gaze met mine and softened, stirring up butterflies in my stomach. "I'll be back soon. Enjoy your meal."

Then he was gone, and I let out a relieved breath. It was like he'd stolen the air away with his mere presence.

Unfortunately, the feeling of relief didn't last long.

Amanda shoved her scrunched-up face in front of mine and growled. Her breath reeked of cheap beer and cigarettes. "Watch your step, pup. Liam isn't available."

A growl tumbled from my own throat, surprising but not stopping me. "You need to take your own advice. Maybe lay off the beer and smokes while you're at it. I could smell your stanky breath from down the stairs."

I had never let anyone bully me growing up—being shorter than most tended to draw the trolls out for some reason. It wasn't like I could control my genetics, for Luna's sake.

Regardless, sometimes I wished I could rein in my sharp tongue. Think before I speak and all that jazz. Now was a perfect example.

She narrowed her eyes into dangerous slits, and her blue irises flashed amber. Her bones rippled beneath her skin, changing shape with grotesque snapping noises. As light brown fur erupted across her face, her nose and mouth elongated.

Still only a few inches from me, she bared her teeth.

Her longer, much sharper teeth.

Oh, shit.

CHAPTER 8

Liam

My jaw cracked from the force of my clenched teeth. What an idiot. I hadn't even noticed Rose's wounds or discomfort from the manacles until I was close enough to touch her.

I'd been too busy gaping like a schoolboy, focused on how good her body looked while covered by a sheet and how the subtle floral spice of moonflowers wrapped around her, enticing me like a gourmet meal. Distracted by how much I loved her spark and the challenge in her stormy gaze.

My wolf rumbled his agreement.

As I strode toward the gate that kept humans out of our village, I slammed my fist into a tree, scarcely noticing the pain shooting through my knuckles. Bark crumbled around my hand, and the trunk groaned in protest before cracking and toppling the rest of the tree over.

Fuck. I needed to get my anger under control. This wasn't alpha behavior—this was me being an asshole.

As the one who fastened the chains too tight, Amanda was clearly jealous of the new wolf. I couldn't blame her. Rose was gorgeous and strong-willed. Mysterious. Every male wolf would be after her.

Warmth slid down my fingers and dripped to the forest floor. The wounds would heal in a matter of minutes, but I clenched my fists, thankful when the gate came into view and forced me to focus on the present.

Sergio and Caleb chatted while they leaned against the rails, both wearing comfortable sweatpants, t-shirts, and backpacks. Standard and inexpensive shifter wear. The two men were distant cousins and shared similar features—black hair, brown eyes, same friendly smile.

But where Caleb's ethnicity was half-Black, Sergio was part-Latino, and his skin was more of a tanned brown with olive undertones. He also loved to wear hipster-style glasses despite having perfect vision.

Sergio's pack, the Massanutten Howlers, had become our rival in recent years before I became the Skyline Pack alpha. Their leader Adrian demanded more land for their increasing numbers, and he wasn't willing to consider any alternatives than just taking it like it was his right.

He was a fool for thinking he was entitled to anything, let alone anything of mine. Our land flourished under the Skyline's care for generations, and I'd be damned before I let a wolf like Adrian destroy it out of greed.

We had lucked out when Sergio approached Caleb, offering to provide information in exchange for a pack to join should things spiral out of control with the Howlers, or if he were caught spying. He didn't like the way Adrian was handling things within his pack, and he wasn't the only one.

Working with him was a no-brainer, win-win scenario for me. Sergio was a great asset either way.

When I reached the gate, I shook his outstretched hand. "You have news?"

"Nope, *nada*. No pack member's been reported missing, and no one matches the description you sent," Sergio said with a shrug.

"I'd say I wish I had more for you, but it's better she's not one of ours."

He wasn't wrong. If she belonged to Adrian's pack, a war would be inevitable if I claimed her as my mate, fated or not. Adrian didn't share anything he considered to be his.

Then again, few alphas did.

"You were careful asking around?"

He shot me an exasperated look over the rim of his glasses. "Come on, does the full moon rise each month?"

I chuckled. "I appreciate your discretion."

"Trust me, anyone would remember Rose," Caleb chimed in and gave a low whistle. "That girl is smokin'."

My muscles rippled beneath my skin as my wolf surged forward, ready to pin Caleb to the ground by the throat to establish our dominance. I hauled my wolf back into line by the metaphorical scruff of his neck.

Caleb laughed and slapped me on the back. "This is going to be a rough month for you, brother."

If my wolf and I wanted to claim her the proper way, the *right* way, then waiting for the next full moon run was a must. Even if she was my fated mate, we had to prove our worth to her, our dominance over any other contenders while Luna smiled down on us.

A month would give us plenty of time to get to know each other and lead to a mutual claiming. That was the goal, but I wasn't so sure my wolf would be okay waiting longer than a month if she needed more time to decide.

Hell, I wasn't sure he would even wait a month. Her wolf would submit willingly, but the woman might not, and that scenario rarely went well.

You know as well as I do that she will, my wolf growled. *Stop lying to yourself.*

Being practical isn't lying. Besides, if she's truly our fated mate, then we're going to have a big *problem on our hands.*

Because destroying my pack was the last thing I would let happen.

Sergio looked between Caleb and me. "I'm guessing your wolf wants to mate with this stranger?"

I rubbed my face with a hand. "You guessed it."

Each time I thought about it, my wolf wanted to run straight to her, bend her over, and claim her. I ground my teeth and held him back.

A long month was a serious understatement.

Sergio and Caleb shared a matching grin, almost smug. I knew what they were thinking, what the entire pack would think once the news got out. Their big bad alpha had a heart after all.

Not that I was an asshole—most of the time—but I ran this pack with discipline and order. Some might say an iron fist, but those were the outliers who caused trouble and picked fights. After the incident with my father, I wasn't taking any chances.

Skyline wolves respected and looked out for one another, and we didn't want for much because of that closeness. There was a reason other packs wanted in and why other alphas followed our successes with curiosity, or envy like Adrian.

A tug at my consciousness meant one of my wolves was looking for me, and I nudged my location back to him. Pack members couldn't communicate with each other outright via telepathy, not like with our own wolves, but general emotions and desires were easy enough to emit.

"Incoming," I said.

We kept Sergio's presence a secret from most of my pack to keep his dual role hidden from Adrian. As luck would have it, he shared a similar peppermint scent to Caleb, which made covering his tracks easier.

With a quick nod, he undressed and stuffed his clothes into his backpack before shifting into his dark brown wolf. He picked up the backpack in his mouth and bounded away.

"Who pinged?" Caleb asked, grinning at my answering glare.

I hated that term and he knew it. A shared pack consciousness should be respected. It wasn't a fucking cell phone. "Damion."

The younger grey wolf padded up a moment later with his tongue hanging out the side of his mouth.

Like most of our pack members, Damion had grown up in this village and only recently became of age to join our hunts and take on a mating scout role. To keep our bloodlines from mixing too closely, we often brought in new wolves during quarterly full moon runs with other packs, as his mother had done.

He'd thrown himself into his new role with enthusiasm, and I respected the hell out of him for it. He would make a fine advisor and father someday.

He shifted back into his two-legged form, standing several inches shorter than Caleb and me. His light brown hair was cut into some sort of a shaggy look he claimed was cool these days, and his dark green eyes always hinted at mischief.

Today, he grinned from ear to ear. "The witches are back."

His grin was contagious. This was our chance to get some answers. "Send out the hunters. I want them caught. No killing."

Damion's disappointment was almost tangible, but the kid—no, he was a man now. Sometimes it was hard to remember that. Regardless, he held his frustration back, ready to obey his alpha.

"Yet," I added with a wink.

His whoop echoed through the trees, startling some nearby birds into flight. He high-fived a laughing Caleb before shifting back into his wolf form and bolting through the trees.

With their ability to teleport, witches could be a pain in the ass to capture, but I wanted answers. I wasn't the only one either. Rose deserved to know why they held her captive and why she couldn't remember anything.

Once we were satisfied with their answers, I'd force one of the bastards to fix her memories.

After that? We would wait and see what Rose wanted to do with them.

There was a possibility she would leave once she knew who she was and where she belonged. It pained me to even consider her leaving, but if she was my fated mate, then it was for the best, no matter how much it hurt.

I wouldn't let my mate destroy my pack like the prophecy said she would.

Remember when you called yourself an idiot? my wolf grumbled. *It's still true.*

We can't put our wants above the pack's needs.

Says who?

Me.

You're no fun.

Never said I was.

Caleb and I headed for the village proper. It wasn't far, so we didn't bother undressing and shifting, but angry shouts soon reached our ears. We exchanged a curious glance and ran the rest of the way.

The ruckus was outside my home, where a circle of riled-up pack members blocked the view of whatever was happening. As I approached, my alpha presence settled over and calmed those watching. They moved to the side to let me through.

In the middle of the crowd, two female wolves circled each other, their lips curled back in angry snarls and their hackles raised. The light brown one lunged and snapped at the other, whose coat was as lily white as her human skin.

Amanda and Rose.

What the fuck had happened in the short time I was gone?

"*Enough.*" Mixed with the word was my alpha command, a dominating force that no pack member could disobey without experiencing extreme pain.

Whimpering, Amanda crouched down, her ears flattened against her head. She shifted to her two-legged form and remained on her knees with her gaze downcast.

Rose didn't appear affected by my command. She wasn't one

of my wolves, but my command should have caused some sort of visible reaction.

Instead, she stared at me in a direct challenge as she shifted back to two legs. Her golden eyes melted into steel grey, and her fur disappeared beneath her skin. Her back straightened until she stood before me with both hands on her shapely hips.

Her naked body glistened with sweat, and her full breasts moved up and down rhythmically, mesmerizing as she caught her breath. Most of her cuts and bruises had healed, but her milky white skin was flushed pink from the fight.

I narrowed my eyes, but a thrill of desire coursed through me. She was so strong and radiant.

My equal.

And I wanted nothing more at that moment than to claim her in front of the pack. Spin her around, bend her over, and teach her to obey her alpha and mate with every delicious thrust. I wanted to grip those hips tight until she screamed my name in ecstasy and submission.

My wolf howled his agreement within our joined thoughts. *I told you you were an idiot for thinking otherwise.*

Her gaze flicked to the front of my jeans, where my arousal strained against the fabric. There was no shame in my reaction to her challenge. She was beautiful and fierce.

Worthy.

It would be a long fucking month indeed.

"Is this how you treat people who've requested sanctuary?" Her demand lashed out as strong as her will. She gestured to Amanda, who rose in a swift movement to get in Rose's face.

The newcomer was about half a foot shorter than Amanda's five foot nine, but she didn't back down. She glared up at the taller woman. "Are you no better than animals?"

Amanda raised her clenched fist to strike.

CHAPTER 9

Rose

"I said enough," Liam's deep voice cracked out like a whip, a command any wolf would be a fool not to follow.

Amazingly, Amanda's fist didn't connect with my face. Which was great because I was over accumulating bruises, and my ankle throbbed again after that fight. Even though her blue eyes blazed with fury and her hand shook from the restraint, she lowered her fist to her side.

"Everyone else is dismissed." His tone required immediate obedience.

The people watching our fight obeyed, though not without a few light grumbles and curious glances shot our way. Caleb was the last to leave, and he shot me a wink over Liam's shoulder. I wasn't sure what that meant, but at least I had one other wolf on my side.

When only the three of us remained, the silence stretched over the area like a smothering blanket. A super awkward silence. Not even the birds called from their trees.

Every living thing waited on pins and needles for the alpha to speak.

Waited for *him*.

"Liam, I—" Amanda began, but Liam cut her off with a look that could probably murder people where they stood.

Yikes. Even in jeans and a t-shirt, this man was terrifying. Yet my body reacted in a completely illogical way—warmth accumulating between my thighs along with a shiver of exhilaration up my spine.

Brushing my long hair forward, I tried to cover some of my flushed skin and rock-hard nipples without drawing attention to my movement. These two might have been used to naked bodily responses, but I wasn't. I wasn't sure I ever would.

I usually felt vulnerable without clothing, and after Josef's disgusting hands groped me before I ran, I wasn't sure I wanted to be naked in front of a man ever again.

Present situation excluded of course, but this was an unfortunate necessity.

Except as Liam's lustful yet appreciative gaze roved over me, I felt powerful. Alive in a way I hadn't realized I'd been missing.

I wanted him to close the distance between us and run those big, strong hands over my body, exploring every inch and curve, touching my most intimate places. Delving deep inside me. A shudder rocked my shoulders.

Yep, I needed to get my hands on some clothes, pronto. Maybe an ice bath, too.

Liam's sharp gaze fixed on Amanda. "One more strike and you're banished from this pack," he growled, his voice low and deep. Barely restrained violence broadcast from his taut muscles like a sound wave.

Shock hit me like the punch I'd escaped only moments before. Great goddess, that was an unexpected response. While I couldn't deny his reaction turned me on hardcore, I also thought it was a bit of an overkill.

The woman had simply misunderstood my intentions, then underestimated *me*. After I'd thrown her down the stairs and out the door, she'd learned her lesson. Liam's arrival only stopped me from proving it to everyone else, too.

He took a menacing step toward her. "I warned you not to disrespect me again. There will be no more second chances after this. I've been far too lenient with you for too long."

Amanda's eyes widened, and her lips parted with a sharp inhale. "You can't be serious."

"Do I look like I'm joking?" He lowered his chin to look directly into her eyes, and she flinched back.

"You would throw away years of friendship?" She gestured wildly at me. "For *her*?"

Well, that was rude, but I knew it was her jealousy talking. That's what this entire fight was about—she thought I was making moves on her man.

First of all, he wasn't my anything. He was a fucking wolf, an animal. Beneath me.

An image of him lying naked beneath me surged forward. His hands clenched around my hips straddling him, his eyes burning with desire as I slid up and down his sizable shaft. Desire for *me*.

Gulping, I tried to ignore the warm tingle that crept down my middle. It wasn't easy.

Second, he most definitely wasn't hers. He had just rocked her whole world with that threat, and not in a good way.

Her nostrils flared, and her narrowed eyes flicked between him and me. She backed away, her steps slow and unsure, and let out a harsh laugh. "You've *got* to be kidding me."

"Don't." Liam took another step toward her, muscles rippling beneath his tanned skin as he tensed.

Not sure what that was about, I rested my hand on his forearm, exhilarating at the spark that flashed through me, at his hard muscles that jumped at my touch.

"Wait." I swallowed down my pride. "Isn't that threat a bit harsh? This was just a misunderstanding between two women."

His body stilled, and he turned those gorgeous blue eyes on me. His stare penetrated me, saw through to my core, and claimed me as his. I didn't know what that meant, or why I didn't run away screaming, but I held firm.

He might have been an alpha, but that didn't make him a god.

Slowly, the tension melted from his shoulders, and his gaze softened. He refocused on Amanda, whose chest heaved with rapid breaths. "I reacted without thinking. I apologize."

He stalked toward her again until he loomed over her, invading her personal space with his dominating presence. "Do not overstep your role within this pack again, or I will find you a new role. One you won't enjoy."

Amanda dropped her gaze, her cheeks blazing red. "Yes, alpha." She escaped while she still could, leaving the two of us alone in the shadows outside his house.

The man that I had to keep reminding myself was an animal swiveled toward me.

My breath hitched as his determined gaze traveled the length of my naked body, and I tightened my muscles to keep from quivering. Everywhere his intense gaze touched, my skin warmed, flushing in more places than my long hair could cover.

He stepped closer, and the warm, rich scent of fir trees drifted toward me, enveloping my senses in pleasure. With each step he took forward, I took one back until the wooden logs of his cabin scratched against my bare back and butt.

Blocking my escape.

His bare toes hit mine, and he raised his hands to either side of my head, his thick, tattooed arms boxing me in. He leaned toward my neck until his warm breath tickled my skin, and his nose brushed against my clavicle.

An electrical current surged outward from his touch, setting off a chain reaction, an inferno through my entire body. I trembled, not wanting him to continue, yet not wanting him to stop either.

I felt like I could hardly breathe, but somehow my chest rose and fell with each harsh breath I sucked in. His blond hair fell forward, obscuring part of his face, and it was all I could do not to reach up and tangle my fingers in those silky strands.

As he dragged his nose up my neck to my ear, inhaling my scent, warmth collected between my thighs. That simple move was intimate, and erotic in a way I'd never thought possible. I dug my nails into the wood behind me, biting back a moan.

"I should punish you, too." His deep voice growled against my ear, and I nearly came undone.

I wanted to beg him to punish me.

"Why?" My voice was barely a whisper, hardly more than a breath. I was almost afraid to speak, afraid he would do it.

More afraid he wouldn't.

"The pack doesn't defy their alpha."

Heat rushed through me as if my body recognized him as my alpha. A ridiculous thought for a witch. I blamed it on the spell hiding me, making me think I was a wolf.

Raising my gaze to meet his, I immediately wished I hadn't. He was so close, I could lick his deliciously full lips from where I stood. I licked mine instead, hoping it would sate my nonsensical desire.

It didn't, and his raw, hungry stare followed my tongue's movement. My heart pounded.

"You're not my alpha," I breathed, not quite sure I believed myself.

The corners of his lips raised, and the slightest hint of dimples appeared on his scruff-covered cheeks. "Not yet."

My sanity slammed back into me like a thunderclap, and I ducked beneath his arm.

I submitted to no man, and certainly not to a wolf.

The fresh air cooled the fire raging beneath my skin, demanding release. "I didn't do anything wrong. She attacked me. I defended myself. It's over."

He dropped his arms from the side of the house and tucked his hands into his jeans pockets. His massive erection strained against the fabric. "Fair enough. You're free to go. I can provide you with a change of clothes and a ride to the nearest town."

My eyebrows shot toward my hairline. Relief settled around me, followed by the unsettling feeling of disappointment. Getting the hell out of here was the best news.

I should be elated.

So, why wasn't I?

"I have to warn you, though," he continued, strolling toward me with a casual, sexy swagger developed from years of confidence, "we've scented the witches on our lands again. They're still looking for you, only now we're hunting them, too."

My breath caught in my throat, afraid of what the witches would do to me if they found me. Beyond terrified at what the wolves would do if they discovered my deception. "Are you going to kill them?"

He tilted his head, and his blue eyes sparkled in the sunlight. "Do you want me to?"

I knew without a doubt he would do exactly that if I asked. This man I'd just met would kill for me. I just didn't know why.

Worse, I liked it. I liked that he even considered my opinion when so many men in his position wouldn't.

"No," I lied.

Okay, it wasn't a complete lie, but better Josef than me.

"Another misunderstanding?" He grinned, revealing his dimples again.

My heart skipped a beat. He'd been so serious since we met, I hadn't thought he was capable of playfulness. It was a really attractive side of him, and I didn't mean just physically. "Something like that."

"I've asked my hunters to capture as many as they can. We all deserve some answers," he said.

My heart skipped again, only this time from bone-chilling fear. If the witches revealed my true identity and that I'd lied to the wolves, deceived *him*, and performed forbidden magic...

...they'd have to take turns ripping me to shreds.

CHAPTER 10

Liam

Rose's body tensed, and indecision flickered across her delicate features, drawing her eyebrows together. My wolf snarled inside us and demanded that I refuse to let her go.

"You're welcome to stay." I kept my tone calm and casual, not wanting to scare her away. I needed to know if she was truly my fated mate, and the only way to know for sure was during the full moon run. "Your memories may return over time, or get shaken loose once you face your captors."

Her haunted gaze met mine, and I had to stop myself from crossing the distance to scoop her into my arms and fight off whatever demons she faced. Real or imagined.

She blinked, and her demons vanished.

A teasing smile crept across her lips, and she raised an eyebrow. "Stay where? In your bed?"

My nostrils flared as sudden need blazed through me and stiffened my already pulsing cock, sending my wolf howling. The image of her naked in my bed—again—was damn near overpowering.

Little did she know, I planned on making that scenario a reality.

Sooner rather than later, preferably. These past twelve hours had been the worst case of blue balls I'd ever experienced. The more time I spent around her, the more I realized I couldn't let her go.

If she turned out to be my fated mate, I would have to pray to Luna the prophecy was wrong. Cecilia's chilling words had haunted me every day for the past year:

"Your fated mate will not be what you expect. Once claimed, she will unite warring factions, or destroy your pack entirely."

How could someone I hardly knew, a woman who appeared so delicate, destroy my pack?

Amanda had scented the raw desire curling off Rose and the mutual reaction coming from me, and rightfully guessed this woman was likely my mate. I didn't want to say anything to Rose until we knew more about her and what Luna had planned for us.

"Caleb's sister has an extra bedroom you can use. She won't mind," I said, finally answering her.

She chewed on her bottom lip in a subconscious sultry look that nearly did me in, and I almost groaned when my dick throbbed. "Okay, but only if she doesn't mind me raiding her closet, too."

A weight lifted from my shoulders, and I released a slow breath. "You'll have anything you need here, just make me a list. For now..." I tugged my shirt over my head and handed it to her. No one but me needed to enjoy the sight of her curves. "Let me show you around."

As her gaze drifted across my bare chest and down to the thick length hidden beneath my jeans, her pupils dilated with desire. She pulled on the shirt, and the bottom hem fell to her thighs, covering the most mouthwatering parts.

The shirt did nothing to stop my raging hard-on, but my scent on her would keep the other males away.

For now.

My wolf growled, bristling. *If they try to make a move, they'll regret it.*

For once on this matter, I agreed.

ROSE

SEEING LIAM SHIRTLESS AGAIN MADE ME RETHINK HIM not being a god. The man's body was unbelievable. His defined muscles were molded into flawless, drool-inducing proportions, rippling with expert control.

He was lethal.

Powerful.

And oh so very sensual.

Thank Luna he turned his back on me just then to point at a path leading away from his house because I licked my lips to catch the drool. My insides clenched and churned, twisting as I fought an insatiable itch that desperately needed to be scratched.

The problem was this man's back was as drool-worthy as his front.

Black ink traveled across his tanned skin, scrollwork patterns blending into a work of art. The lines came together between his sharp shoulder blades where a wolf howled at the full moon. The workmanship was exquisite.

Unable to resist the urge, I reached out to trace the ink with my fingers.

With a single touch, lightning danced across my skin and spread like wildfire. His body tensed, corded muscles undulating beneath my fingers until I snatched my hand away. There was no denying he felt the spark, too.

Taking a few steps down the path, Liam glanced over his shoulder at me. Desire smoldered in his gaze. "Coming?"

"Not yet," I grumbled under my breath, too low for him to hear. My body clenched in a frustrating reminder, and I hurried after him.

To be honest, I looked forward to seeing the rest of the wolves' village. A sick curiosity, if you will, considering their preference to live like wild animals. Like savages.

Plus, it would be an excellent distraction for my raging lady boner.

All my life, my parents had taught me that shapeshifters were the lowest of all the supernatural beings in our world, lower even than humans. They'd told me countless stories about the ferocious predators who hunted our kind in the night, devouring children and even babies.

My parents would spin in their graves if they knew where I had ended up. What a dumpster fire of a disaster my life had become.

I followed Liam along the winding dirt trail through the trees. When the path ended at an expansive graveled courtyard area, I stopped and gaped in surprise.

An enormous two-story log cabin with a green gabled roof stretched out before us. It was at least as long as a football field and took up the majority of the cleared space, though smaller structures peeked out from behind the cabin and from in between trees.

Smoke drifted up from the cabin's multiple chimneys, blending seamlessly with the puffs of clouds in an otherwise blue sky. The warm, earthy smell mixed with the local flora and fauna, creating a rich yet comforting scent. Butterflies and buzzing bees flitted among the grass and flowers edging the gravel roads.

Other dirt paths wound away from this central area and through the surrounding forest, and people and wolves went about their daily business.

The view was unbelievably picturesque and so unlike what I'd expected. It was unlike anything I'd ever heard about the wolves, and confusion tightened my chest. For all I knew, this was unusual for wolf life.

A few fully dressed people waved or nodded to Liam as we continued toward the central building. I tugged on the hem of my shirt, wishing I wasn't so filthy or had on some pants—or, you know, underwear.

I hadn't had a chance to shower, which meant I was still covered in dirt, sweat, and blood, and my hair had lost its glossy shine. Not that I cared what the wolves thought of me, but I had standards for being seen in public, no matter where I was.

No one seemed to notice or care about my disastrous appearance, though. They looked at me with curiosity, and I guessed my lack of clothes and disheveled state wasn't altogether unexpected or surprising to a pack of wolves. They likely spent most of their time outdoors rolling in the mud.

"This is our communal hall." Liam placed his hand on the small of my back as we approached three steps leading up to the wide porch. Even through the shirt, his touch branded my skin, scorching down to my toes.

It wasn't pure physical attraction, either. His gesture was chivalrous, speaking to a time I'd considered long forgotten by men my age. I had a sneaking suspicion he was the type to hold open car doors, too.

He didn't remove his hand as we entered the two open front doors, and it was all I could do to focus on my surroundings and not the blissful warmth spreading through my body.

Rows and rows of wooden picnic tables took up the majority of the central interior. Along the right wall, a bustling community kitchen served buffet-style food to anyone who walked up. On the opposite side, small shops and stalls offered various grocery items and personal products.

My eyebrows drew together as I took in the scene and processed it. The atmosphere and daily activities seemed so... normal. Like any normal day in my life and very unlike the descriptions my parents had painted of wolf life.

In their stories, shapeshifting wolves lived in dens or crudely made huts. They preferred raw meat gnawed straight off the bone after a fresh kill. They bathed in rivers and creeks once a month, if that.

I wondered whether my parents had ever stepped foot in a wolves' village, or if this place was simply unique.

At the far end of the picnic tables, a group of men and women with wrinkled skin and grey and white hair sat in rocking chairs near a crackling fireplace. A few younger people attended to their needs with friendly yet respectful gestures and kind smiles.

I nearly laughed in surprise when I spied a few wolves with their eyes closed, snoozing beside the elders' feet. Lighter fur along their muzzles indicated they were likely as old as the people in the chairs.

Dozens of people of all ages came and went, browsing the goods available in the market area or sitting at tables while they ate and chatted. A line of five pups with wagging tails trailed behind a larger brownish-grey wolf and disappeared down a hall.

I couldn't believe how many pack members there were inside this one building. My skin prickled with goosebumps. I was surrounded by so many wolves...

My mortal enemies.

If any one of them were to discover I was a witch in wolves' clothing, I'd never make it out alive. Fitting in and staying under the radar would be a must, as was getting the hell away from here as soon as possible.

"Anything seem familiar?" Liam asked, his mouth close to my ear, startling me.

I shook my head, thankful for the interruption of my thoughts. My heart continued to pound so loud, I was sure he would hear it. "Do all your pack towns have halls like this?"

He glanced around. "Some, though usually not this big. Most of my pack lives here, though, with only a few smaller communities in the surrounding area."

"Is that normal for packs? To have most of them living near the alpha?"

His blue eyes focused on me, and heat rose in my cheeks. I hoped I wasn't being curious to the point of giving myself away. I didn't actually know how amnesia worked for this kind of stuff.

Or, you know, at all.

Hopefully most people here hadn't studied amnesia either.

"It's a common practice," he said, and I breathed a small sigh of relief. "Alphas provide their packs with protection, so staying close makes most wolves feel safe."

I nodded and picked at the shirt's hem. "Do they sell clothes here?"

He grinned, flashing those scruff-covered dimples that would make most women's panties melt off. Sadly, I was no exception, but panties were a luxury I didn't get to enjoy just yet.

"Don't worry about that." He motioned me toward a side door leading back outside. "We don't use money here, but I'll cover anything you need while you stay."

"I can't let you do that..." my voice trailed away as we stepped outside, and my lips parted with a small gasp.

The most amazing garden I'd ever seen spread out over a cleared plot that must have covered several acres, with ample unused space for growth. Raised beds and orchards were protected with wire, keeping the clucking, pecking chickens roaming the area from destroying the plants.

Farther out, cows and sheep gathered in small herds and flocks, milling about or lowering their mouths to the grass for a snack. Barn roofs poked above the trees, and people strode in and out as they went about their chores or jobs.

"Wow," was all I could manage.

"Impressive isn't it?" His soft tone spoke volumes of his pride over this work of art, and he nodded to the handful of people working the fields and tending to the animals. "Most of our food comes from this labor of love, and it gives us something to trade and barter with."

"With who? Other packs?" I asked with genuine curiosity.

"Other packs or nearby human towns. We try to remain self-sufficient and limit interactions, but some things are easier to buy than make." He pointed toward the solar panels covering the building's roof on this side. "We have phones and internet, but cell signals have never been great out here."

Such a difference between their lives and mine. Even during the retreat at Josef's, we had enjoyed so many creature comforts, yet these wolves seemed perfectly content with less. Happier and not weighed down by city-living stress.

My chest felt lighter here than it had over the last year since my parents died. Maybe even ever, and the feeling confused the hell out of me. I felt like I belonged.

I returned my attention to the garden beds. My fingers itched to dig into the dirt and nourish the life growing there. "I've always been good with plants. I'd love to help out to make up for whatever I use."

He turned a curious gaze on me and raised his eyebrows. "Memories coming back?"

Crap. I almost ruined my entire amnesiac façade with one simple statement. Before he could see the truth in my eyes, I looked away and gestured to the tomato trellises, covered in vines. "I can remember how much I love gardening, and they say memories are made from emotions, right?"

I knew he was still looking at me, and my cheeks flushed beneath his intense stare. He drew in a breath to speak, but whatever he was about to say was cut off by an unfamiliar woman's voice.

"And just what do we have here?"

CHAPTER 11

Rose

I leaned forward to see who'd spoken behind Liam's giant form. A tall, slender woman stood with her arms crossed.

She looked almost exactly like Caleb but with long, curly black hair and more delicate, feminine features. Her light brown skin was smooth and flawless, and she had one eyebrow arched dramatically.

Black linen shorts poked out from beneath a blue tunic-length tank top, and black Birkenstock-style sandals covered her feet.

"Thanks for coming, Mal," Liam said, his deep voice softening with obvious affection.

I shot a glance at his face, unease tickling my stomach.

Who was this woman to him?

She uncrossed her arms and sauntered closer, her dark brown gaze examining me like a hawk. No, like a wolf. "As the alpha ordered."

"Rose, this is Mallory, Caleb's twin sister," he explained. "We don't know Rose's real name, but the tattoo provided something to use for now."

Her gaze flicked to the rose on my ankle, and she smirked. "How typical. I'm guessing you got it in college?"

Anger flushed through me. I was pretending to have amnesia, which meant I couldn't reveal the truth about what the thorny rose meant to me. How my mother's teasing yet loving words about my name would stay with me forever.

Rooming with this woman might have been a terrible idea. I pasted on a smile. "Probably."

Based on her lack of surprise about my name, it was safe to assume Liam had already told her my story. What little there was to share, anyway.

"Alright, I got her from here, big man." She shooed him away with a hand. "Go do some important alpha things."

My nostrils flared, and I had to bite my tongue to keep from snapping at her. Sure, he had more important things to do than babysit me, but I hated the insinuation that I wasn't important to him.

Or maybe I was jealous of her comfort level with him.

Either way, I needed to cool it. Nothing would come from this weird attraction I had to a wolf.

Liam hesitated briefly before nodding. "I appreciate it." His fingers brushed against mine intimately before he lifted my hand and kissed the back of it. His blue eyes sparkled as he met my gaze. "You'll be in good hands, Rose. See you tonight."

Butterflies didn't just tickle my stomach—they danced a lively jig. The instinctual act of breathing became difficult, and each struggling inhale made my heart beat faster.

Letting my hand go as if it were the last thing he wanted to do, he backed away slowly. With a wink that made my stomach flip-flop, he rounded the community hall's corner, disappearing from view.

"Girl, you got it bad." Mallory's amused voice snapped me back to reality.

I pressed my hands to my flaming cheeks. Maybe I was reading too much into his somewhat romantic gesture, but I was pretty sure he'd just made it clear that he and Mallory weren't a thing. "I don't know what you mean."

She let out a short laugh. "Mmhm. Whatever you say. Follow me. You need a hot shower and some proper clothes, like, yesterday."

I couldn't agree with her more.

As we made our way back down the path from earlier, I realized that Mallory's house wasn't far from Liam's, as in visible from her porch. A fact that made my insides squish for a few reasons that didn't make any sense.

I shouldn't care how close the man lived to Mallory, and I definitely shouldn't care that he would be so close to me while I stayed here, which wouldn't be long. Once the coast was clear of my coven, I was gone.

Mallory's quaint one-story cabin had a sloped green roof, a wrap-around front porch complete with a porch swing, and a small shed peeking out around the back. I followed her up the steps and inside, which turned out to be just as adorable as the outside.

A cozy living room fed into the corner kitchen in an open-concept layout, and a tiny table hugged the wall and window between the two areas. Dotted throughout the space in painted pots, flowers and creeping vines cast off a lovely floral smell. Straight ahead, a short hallway led into the back of the home.

"You won't get lost here," Mallory said and pointed to the hall. "First door's mine, bathroom's second, third's yours. Go get that stench off while I fix you a quick bite. You'll find toiletries in the bathroom and fresh clothes on your bed."

She wasted no time heading for the kitchen, leaving me standing with moisture gathering in my eyes. So far, these wolves were treating me like an honored guest, not like an enemy or as little more than a means for making cubs like in the horror stories I'd grown up hearing.

Plus, my first impression of Mallory had been dead wrong. I'd only just met this woman, and she had opened up her home to me without complaint. She even called her things mine, as if I were moving in forever.

She had no way of knowing she'd just invited in her enemy, but I wasn't so sure she'd treat me any differently if she knew the truth.

Contrary to what my parents had taught me and what the coven believed, these wolves were just people, with friends and families and *jobs*, for goddess's sake. They were the farthest thing from the monsters I'd expected.

Feeling like everything I'd been told was a lie, I swallowed down the lump forming in my throat.

Who were the real animals, these people?

Or the witch who was stealing magic from his own kind and robbing them of their memories?

Before Mallory could turn around and see me about to break down, I hustled for the hallway. Three closed doors on the left greeted me. I headed for the second and locked the door behind me.

Pressing my back to the closed door, I gulped down deep breaths, trying to calm my racing pulse and swirling vision. A curtain fluttered in front of a cracked window. I raced to it, pushing it open more and sucking in the fresh air like I was drowning.

When the panic subsided and I was sure I wouldn't pass out, I turned on the shower as hot as it could go. I pulled the oversized shirt over my head and held it to my nose, breathing in the fir scent.

His scent.

Shivering, I dropped the shirt on the floor as if it were a snake. Less than a day with the wolves and I was already acting like one.

The once-white t-shirt was now streaked with dirt and blood, and I wrinkled my nose. I should probably burn the thing and save him the laundry hassle.

I stepped into the scalding water and scrubbed away last

night's mad dash through the woods until the water circling the drain changed from ruddy brown to clear. Not wanting to leave the warmth yet, I let the water run down my back and the steam soak into my pores.

The memory of Liam leaning close, his nose sliding up my neck, rose unbidden. His tanned forearms had glistened with a light sweat as he moved in, his sculpted muscles twitching from the slow, controlled movement.

Closing my eyes, I slid a hand down my stomach, between my legs, and slipped a finger inside. No big surprise—I was already soaking wet, and not from the shower.

When Liam had me caged against the logs between his huge arms, his blue eyes had darkened with desire. There was no denying that he wanted me, wanted to be inside me just as much as I wanted him.

While I stroked deeper with my finger, I rubbed myself with my thumb, biting my lip as the need to release built slowly.

I imagined him here with me now, naked, rivulets of water snaking their way down the lines of his sculpted chest and abs. His long blond hair would darken as it got wet, and his lust-filled gaze would penetrate my soul.

His massive erection, so smooth and perfectly shaped, would lengthen and thicken until it was as hard as a rod, ready to impale itself deep inside me.

My breaths grew rapid and shallow in the steam as my orgasm neared. I pressed my lips together to hold back a moan as I slid a second finger inside.

He would kneel before me, his hands moving up my slick body, and drape one of my legs over his shoulder. Then his warm breath would flutter over my core just before he parted my folds with his tongue.

Licking and sucking, he would thrust and curl his fingers inside me, again and again until...

Until...

"Fuck," I gasped out as an intense orgasm gripped me. My legs threatened to collapse beneath me, and I grabbed the built-in soap holder for dear life as my body shuddered.

A rap at the door made me yelp. I slammed my elbow into the tile wall in my attempt not to fall out of the shower and winced as a sharp pain spasmed up my arm.

"Rose?" Mallory's voice called through the wood. "Just making sure you didn't pass out or something."

"Nope, just dirty. *Very* dirty," I called back, rubbing my elbow. If only she knew exactly how dirty. "Finishing up now."

Seriously, what the hell was wrong with me?

Yes, he was a physically attractive, strong man with some gentlemanly moves that made my body tingle. Remembering his soft touch when he removed the chains and his big hand pressed against my back as he led me around the village brought a new heat to my cheeks.

Sighing in frustration, I turned the knob to cold and gasped as the water doused my still-simmering inner fire. I shut off the shower and grabbed a towel, grumbling at my poor timing for releasing some tension, with images of *him*, no less.

Being a super sexy gentleman didn't make him any less of a wolf.

An alpha.

I'd hardly spent any time with him or any others, but it was clear his pack respected him. All except that Amanda chick, anyway, but she seemed like an outlier.

Oh, who was I kidding? What did I even know about wolves and pack life? Maybe they were all putting on a show, trying to make me believe they were better, more civilized than they truly were.

I scrunched up my nose as I dried off. Except that made no sense. No one here knew I was a witch, or anything other than another wolf. They had no reason to pretend to be anything but themselves.

When I was no longer dripping, I wrapped the towel around myself and padded down the hall to the third door.

Inside, Mallory had furnished the room with a full-sized bed flanked by side tables and a dresser. Another door led out to the wrap-around porch, and lace curtains covered two windows. Spotting a tank top and leggings on the bed, I smiled.

I had run from a nightmare only to end up here, a place I once thought of as the real nightmare. I approached the bed, bewildered.

Taken in by a wolf pack with hospitality skills I'd only read about in fiction books. Provided a place to sleep, clothes, and food without anyone asking for anything in return.

Maybe I'd knocked my head harder than I thought and was still passed out in the woods. Or maybe I'd never actually cast the spell but got eaten by wolves, and this was the afterlife.

The spell...

My hand flattened against my naked chest, and my eyes widened.

Oh, no.

The necklace—it was gone.

CHAPTER 12

Rose

After dressing in a hurry, I squeezed out as much excess water from my hair as I could. My heart thudded harder with every passing moment. Losing the charm hadn't even occurred to me when I cast the spell.

Thanks to the fight with Amanda, I already knew I could shapeshift without it, but I needed to get my necklace as soon as possible. If a wolf found it before I did and discovered its purpose, I'd be dead before nightfall.

I rushed out of the room and into the main living area, where Mallory sat on a comfortable-looking chair next to the couch. "Can you show me where I was found?"

She looked up from her magazine with a raised eyebrow. "Why?"

"I feel like I left something behind," I said, furrowing my eyebrows and trying to sound confused. Playing dumb was harder than I thought it'd be. "Maybe whatever it is will jog my memories loose."

"Food first." She nodded to the sandwich waiting on the kitchen island. "And Liam would want to know before we leave."

My heart dropped as I approached the island. As much as my

body enjoyed the man's presence, I also found it much harder to focus around him. I might give myself away without even realizing it.

"Good thing I don't usually care what he wants." She winked.

After a brief moment of surprise, I laughed and grabbed the plate. I was a fool for ever thinking we wouldn't get along.

Nearly groaning out loud with the first bite, I inhaled the turkey sandwich in record time. Thanks to everything that had occurred since waking up, I hadn't realized how hungry I was.

When I finished, Mallory put her magazine down on the coffee table and stood. "A run would be good for our wolves. Think you've got it in you?"

My heart soared. "Absolutely."

Following her lead, I removed my clothes and shifted into a white wolf—a process that was far less painful today than last night, thank the goddess. I trailed Mallory's grey wolf outside and into the forest.

Running on two legs and faster than any human had always been exhilarating and resulted in a full-ride scholarship to college.

But running as a wolf?

It was...

Indescribable.

Everything around us passed in a blur like we were flying across the ground. I was hardly even aware of my surroundings, yet somehow avoided any obstacle and kept pace with Mallory easily.

Giddiness lifted my spirits, and I felt like I could run forever. Sadly, it was over much too soon.

Mallory slowed as the sound of rushing water reached my ears, and I recognized the steep ravine I'd tumbled down. The grey wolf trotted over to a grassy clearing and touched the ground with her nose before looking at me.

Not that she needed to point it out. My ripped clothes were strewn about, never to be worn again. Spying a piece of my favorite shirt from high school, a twinge of sorrow passed through me.

It was a silly reaction, really. I should have tossed the shirt ages ago when the band's logo had finally faded into obscurity. My dad had taken me to that concert, and when I cleaned out our townhouse after my parents' deaths, I hadn't been able to part with the shirt.

I had no family waiting for me after all this, no siblings or distant aunts or uncles, not even a best friend anymore. I was alone.

My previous life was officially over.

Swallowing the intense emotions to process another day, I padded over to Mallory and sniffed the grassy area. I'd have better luck with heightened wolfish senses than my own.

Unfortunately, wolfish senses did little to help a lost cause. An hour later, our thorough search in both forms proved fruitless.

The necklace had vanished.

Claiming exhaustion, I spent the few remaining hours of sunlight in Mallory's guest room. My room, for the time being.

In reality, I was trying to cast a locating spell. Scratch that, I was failing to cast a simple locating spell.

Simple when I had the proper items, at any rate. The room had a scented candle in a glass jar, and I found a matchbox in a bedside table's drawer. But I still needed a map of the area.

I'd attempted the spell without it by visualizing a map in my head to no avail, and my single attempt at drawing one on the bedspread with even simpler magic had almost resulted in a fire. A tiny charred mark in the fabric would remain as permanent evidence of my crime.

Hopefully she wouldn't notice.

A knock at the door startled me so badly, the candle's hot wax splashed onto my arm. I bit back a yelp and dissolved the millionth failed spell just as the knob turned and the door opened.

Mallory stuck her head in. "Good, you're up. It's dinner time."

Holy mother goddess, that had been close. If she hadn't knocked first, she would have caught me in the act. The only light in the room came from my candle, which had made the wisps of glowing magic all the more obvious.

Wanting to try again, I opened my mouth to decline, but my rumbling stomach beat me to the punch.

She raised her eyebrows and smirked. "You're too petite for such a monstrous sound." Her gaze flicked from the candle in my hand to the wax solidifying on my arm. "Finish up your kinky solo sesh then meet me out front."

My mouth dropped open, but she was gone before I could babble out another excuse. Groaning, I set the candle down and peeled off the wax.

With my luck, Mallory would mention the assumed wax kink to her brother, who would tell Liam, who would most definitely look at me in another light. A sexier light, maybe, but I wasn't into that sort of thing.

I pursed my lips and considered the wax for a moment. Nope, I wasn't into that, and I wasn't into wolves. Period.

Sighing, I went to meet Mallory. Women's voices drifted through the open front door but their faces were virtually invisible. Night had fallen, bathing the outside world in darkness.

As I left the house, a passing cloud drifted away, and bright moonlight fell across the visitor's face. I stopped short on the top step.

Amanda's sharp blue gaze stabbed into mine. "A wolf who claims she lost her memories is a pretty fucking convenient excuse right now."

My anger flared like a struck match.

Mallory made a sound of disgust. "Better than a wolf who doesn't know her place."

Oh, I liked her even more now. Without another glance at Amanda, I skipped down the steps and approached Mallory. "You mentioned dinner?"

Amanda snarled and stepped in front of me. "Ignoring me won't end well for you, little pup."

I rolled my eyes. "Making fun of my height? That's original."

"Let it go, Amanda." Mallory slid between us with her hands up. Which was good timing because I was pretty sure Amanda's reddening face was a sign she was about to punch me. "Liam says she's welcome here. You don't want me to tell the alpha you're disobeying his command, do you?"

The other woman's fury-filled gaze bored into mine for another moment before she took a step back. No, she didn't want to press her luck and find herself with a new role or be banished from the pack.

"One wrong move and you're mine." The hint of instability in her tone sent a chill down my spine. "Better watch your back."

She didn't have to tell me twice. Practicing magic, even in the safety of my room, would be a hard nope after that threat.

As Mallory took my arm to lead me away, I glanced over my shoulder and swallowed hard. Prickles crept across my scalp.

Although Amanda had vanished into the shadows, her lingering hatred burned into my back.

CHAPTER 13

Liam

Before I knew it, a week had passed, and my wolf was getting even more restless than usual. It was probably because I wasn't letting Amanda into my bed anymore, but that was too fucking bad for him.

The only woman I wanted to bury myself in was Rose.

Oh, goddess, I wanted her so fucking bad, wanted to claim her as my mate and my lover. I wanted her writhing beneath me, moaning and gasping as I rammed into her sweet warmth, unrelenting until she shattered and screamed my name.

I leaned against a tree in the forest's dark shadows and clenched my jaw, willing my vision to focus on the bonfire and not the inferno raging through my veins. If I had my way, I would have plenty of time to explore the unbelievable curves of her body.

Just not tonight.

Tonight was Caleb and Mallory's birthday, and as usual, the Skyline Pack celebrated around the bonfire. Most of our birthdays were celebrated by grilling meat, roasting marshmallows, and drinking long into the night. Balloons and cakes were more of a human tradition.

Laughter and music rose into the sky, drifting toward the

bright stars on roads of billowing smoke. Charring steak teased my senses, and my mouth watered even from the distance I maintained.

Despite what humans wrote in their stories about shapeshifters, we only enjoyed raw meat in our wolf forms, but the tantalizing scent only added to the difficulty of my current situation. I was aroused and hungry in more ways than one as I watched Rose interact with my pack.

I'd thought she was gorgeous covered in dirt and blood, her hair wild like a frenzied maenad, but I had severely underestimated her beauty. She was radiant, glowing like a goddess.

Her long hair shone beneath the moonlight and against the flickering flames, so black it appeared blue. It was thick and glossy and, combined with tonight's black crop top and high-waisted leggings that emphasized her curves, her flawless skin appeared even whiter in contrast.

A week without trouble from the witches had helped her heal, and her steel grey eyes sparkled with teasing delight every time we met. But every day that she stayed became an annoying blend of relief and fear.

There was no denying she was beyond beautiful in looks, but it was her confident, fiery personality that melted my frozen heart as no one else had. The rest of the pack had been quick to accept her presence around the village, and she'd taken an active role in tending to the community gardens.

I was thrilled she'd stayed this long, but each night, I slept uneasily, concerned it would be her last. Worried she would leave the village with the rising sun.

Terrified she'd leave *me*.

She tossed her head back, laughing at something Mallory had said, and the sound of her unrestrained happiness caressed my soul and soothed my restless wolf. I could live the rest of my days hearing nothing but that laugh and die a very happy old wolf.

Unfortunately, I wasn't the only one who noticed how special she was. Every eligible single male—and even a few of the older ones—had eyed her over the last week, infuriating my wolf. I didn't blame him; I desired her as much as he did. But he didn't want to play by civilized rules.

I heard that, he grumbled.

Good, I said. *Whatever she went through before falling into our lap, she deserves better from us.*

A young yet eligible male named Smith approached Rose with a drink, and her smile dazzled us both. When she laughed at whatever he said and touched his arm, I almost lost it. Growling, I gripped the tree's trunk, and my claws extended and sank into the bark.

Her gaze moved around the bonfire, searching beneath furrowed eyebrows. I was too far for anyone to have heard my reaction, but I knew she had sensed my sudden emotion, just as I sensed hers more each day.

No matter where I was, her presence called to me. Her scent teased me, her growing desire begging me to claim her. I was sure the other males scented her arousal, a thought that triggered me more than I cared to admit.

Caleb's peppermint and pine scent approached, though his steps were silent from years of training. There were herbs and tinctures we could ingest to hide our scents, but we never wasted the effort or resources within our community's boundaries.

"Thought I'd find you here," he said.

My vision swam red with rage. Smith had taken Rose's hand and spun her around, earning a joyous laugh before he drew her close for a dance. I ripped my claws free of the tree, sending bark flying, and took a step toward the bonfire.

Prophecy be damned.

She was *mine*.

"Whoa, brother." Caleb popped up in front of me, his hands raised to stop me. "Before you go on a murderous rampage, we gotta talk. Pack problems."

I closed my eyes and inhaled, letting the cool night air filter through me and calm my racing pulse. As much as I wanted to prove my dominance over Smith as a mate, the pack needed to come first. Tonight was not the night.

"What is it?" My tone was harsher than I intended, but Caleb would understand.

"Amanda."

My eyelids snapped open, and I glared at him. "What now?"

Ever since the first incident with Rose, Amanda's insolence had gotten worse. As one of my pack advisors, her behavior with me had always been far too personal and relaxed, a problem I should have corrected months ago.

Thank Luna she was on patrol tonight.

Caleb sighed. "What hasn't she done, man? She's a sore loser. Every chance she gets, she antagonizes Rose, trying to pick another fight. Rose ignores her for the most part, but eventually, one of 'em's gonna snap."

I clenched my teeth. I hadn't seen any incidents myself, but Rose's nervousness whenever Amanda was around made even more sense now. "She'll learn to control herself or she'll find herself banished. This time for real."

I should have ripped off the bandaid the first time Amanda had gone after her. Against my better judgment, I hadn't been able to say no to Rose, and now, we were both paying the price.

"Do you still think she's your fated mate?" Caleb asked, his gaze focused on the bonfire.

I knew he meant Rose. "At this point, without a doubt."

There was no other explanation for our sensing each other's emotions and closeness. Fated mates had a unique bond unlike regular mating, and it solidified once the pair claimed each other.

He nodded and crossed his arms. "She's a good choice, far better than Amanda."

While I couldn't agree more, there was just one problem. One huge fucking problem. "If I claim her, it'll set the prophecy in motion. She'll destroy our pack."

Then she'll destroy me.

Leave the prophecies to the humans, my wolf said dismissively.

You know as well as I do how accurate Cecilia's visions are.

Yet she struggles to interpret them, just like anyone else, he said.

Caleb scoffed. "You put too much faith in an old woman's rumblings." He held up a hand before I could protest. "Yeah, okay, she's been right more often than not, but she's also been wrong. Or we've misinterpreted the message. Same could be true now."

Grinning, he smacked my arm. "Cecilia said your fated mate *may* destroy the pack, but she could just as easily unite our 'warring factions.'"

His comments were right in line with my wolf's, but prophecies were open to interpretation, and more commonly, misinterpretation. Neither Caleb nor my wolf was admitting the full truth. Cecilia had only been wrong once, and my parents had learned that the hard way—with their lives.

"We don't want a war," he continued. "So claim her during the full moon, and whatever happens, we'll find a way through. We always do." He put his hand on my shoulder and gave me a shake. "Either way, you gotta stop brooding, man. The pack senses it. It's my birthday, so have some fun tonight. Oh, and she's been looking for you."

As usual, my beta had turned my attitude around and distracted me from doing something rash, like throwing Smith into the woods in front of everyone or moving Amanda to another village within our pack.

While that last idea sounded promising, it wouldn't resolve the root cause of her issues. Besides, she was an excellent advisor when she wanted to be.

I walked with Caleb back to the party and accepted the drink someone offered. The pack enjoyed seeing their alpha let loose every once in a while, but I never lost control. Not from alcohol at any rate.

A tingling sensation crawled up my back, and I turned to find Rose's attention fixed on me over her cup. Desire blazed within her eyes, and a flush crept into her cheeks and across the swell of her breasts.

As her gaze trailed down my body, she licked her lips in a seemingly involuntary reaction, one I understood all too well. My body responded in kind, my dick stiffening beneath her hungry stare.

When she finally met my gaze, I smiled and raised my cup in acknowledgment.

The pink tint in her cheeks deepened, but she copied my gesture before returning her attention to Mallory. My cock twitched, and I adjusted my stance to give it more room.

Three more weeks and she would be mine, even if claiming her destroyed the pack.

Even if she ruined me.

CHAPTER 14

Rose

I tried to focus on what Mallory was saying, really and truly I did, but my pulse thudded in my ears, drowning out everything else. My head and thoughts were fuzzy as every inch of my body tingled with insatiable desire.

Only a week had passed since I first arrived and met Liam, but it felt like a lifetime.

A lifetime of absolute, exquisite torture.

I didn't sleep around by any means, but I sure as shit wasn't a virgin or celibate either. This ongoing sexual tension thing was driving me crazy. Mostly because I didn't know why I reacted so wantonly around him, or why my traitorous body craved his presence whenever he was gone.

Making it worse was his undeniable attraction to me, as well as his refusal to do anything about it. For the most part, he was the perfect gentleman.

When he wasn't being a total, domineering alpha, that is. A shiver slid up my spine. He could dominate me any day.

Nope. Nuh-uh. Not going there.

My hand only provided so much relief—I needed a big dick inside me pronto. The problem was there was only one such big dick I wanted at the moment, and that wasn't happening for a variety of reasons.

"Seriously, Rose?" Mal's exasperated tone snapped my attention back to reality and her dramatically arched eyebrow.

She'd straightened her black hair, and it hung long and loose down her back. Black leather pants hugged her ass and thighs tight, showing off her toned muscles beneath, and a blood-red cropped blouse looked amazing next to her light brown skin.

While her usual preference was no shoes or comfortable sandals, tonight she'd slipped on a pair of matching red heels. In her own words, she was on the prowl and ready to howl.

I winced. "Sorry. What'd you say?"

"What I said doesn't matter, but girl, you have got to get laid." She glanced over her shoulder at Liam, who thankfully wasn't facing our way anymore, then shot me a knowing smirk.

Already warm from the fire—among other reasons—my cheeks flushed even more. "Is it that obvious?"

"Everyone can smell your arousal when you're around him," she said with a devious grin. "No one else is going to touch you while he's present. So make that shit happen."

I groaned. Well, that was inconvenient and embarrassing. Wish I'd known that fantastic tidbit from the start.

Unfortunately for my strung-out body, high and vibrating on unsatisfied sexual tension, I was not going to make that shit happen. I hadn't tracked down my necklace yet, and without it, my façade would be up at the next full moon.

The more I realized I had no one else to turn to, no family or friends to take me in, my opinion about leaving as soon as possible had changed. I would stay until I devised a plan to free the witches Josef held captive.

But if I didn't find the charm in the next few weeks, I would have no choice except to leave, my body's needs be damned.

Besides, the asshole alpha hadn't even made a move. Not to

mention he was a wolf, a fact I conveniently forgot more and more often.

My parents would rise from their graves and haunt me if I didn't get a grip soon.

I took a sip of my beer, wishing I hadn't let it get so warm. I needed an ice bath. "He avoids me like the plague."

"Not for the reason you think," Mallory said.

Before I could ask what that reason was, her friends whisked her away for another round of beer pong. I'd been able to avoid any games so far, but the crowd was getting rowdier, and I was sure my luck wouldn't last much longer.

The last thing I needed was to get so drunk that I did something stupid.

Or more likely did some*one*.

I downed the last of my drink, chucked the cup into the trash, then slipped away. I didn't want to be rude by leaving early, but I was also pretty sure no one would notice my absence. They were all too far gone.

The moon was still in its third quarter, reflecting more than enough sunlight to bathe the path ahead in a soft white glow. Crickets trilled, and nightly critters scurried through the underbrush or flitted through the trees.

A branch hung low over the path, and I reached up to caress the leaves. I smiled as they recognized me and leaned into my touch despite the spell camouflaging my essence from the pack. I'd always loved the woods and camping, but there was something special about these trees.

Witches had a natural attunement to all plants in general. We worked together in harmony, witches encouraging growth and healing within the plant and receiving a bounty of leaves, berries, and seeds for potions in return. A symbiotic relationship that I cherished and missed.

"Heading home already?"

Startled, I dropped my hand and whirled around, meeting Liam's blue eyes. The color was visible even in the limited light.

I hadn't even heard him approach. Had he seen how the tree greeted me?

He'd pulled his blond hair back into a low ponytail tonight, providing an unobscured view of his whole face for the first time since we'd met. The strong lines of his jaw were more visible after his recent shave, and I longed to run my fingers across his smooth skin.

I settled for clasping my hands behind my back. "I'm still getting used to the bigger crowds."

He smiled, flashing his adorable, panty-soaking dimples. "I'll walk with you."

We strolled side by side, close enough for me to feel his heat, but not close enough to touch. Neither of us spoke, which was good because I didn't trust anything proper to come out of my mouth right now. Especially not after the few drinks I'd had.

I wasn't sure if I wanted to scream at him for somehow making me feel this way, or throw myself at him and demand he satisfy my needs.

It could really go either way tonight.

When we reached Mallory's house, I skipped up the few steps leading to her porch and front door, and my heart beat faster. We were alone and so close to my bed or the couch. The kitchen counter would work right now.

Hell, even the steps could prove interesting.

Considering how strong my reaction was, he had to feel the same way. If nothing else, Mallory had just revealed he could smell my arousal, along with the rest of the pack.

Which meant this was it. The moment I'd been waiting for.

No, make that *dying* for.

At the bottom of the steps, he stopped, tucking his hands into his jeans pockets. The casual pose made him even sexier. "You seem to like it here."

"That's because I do." The admission came out without hesitation and surprised me. It was the truth, too, and not entirely because of the man standing in front of me.

I'd begrudgingly accepted the fact that my parents and my coven had been wrong. Shapeshifters were far more than just animals who lived out their lives by following their basic instincts.

In reality, they weren't too different from humans and witches. Maybe not so different from any other supernatural group, either, though I hadn't come across any others yet. That I knew of, anyway. We were all adept at hiding among humans.

Liam's blue eyes twinkled beneath the porch light. "I'm glad to hear it. Any memories coming back?"

"Fuzzy images but nothing firm yet." The fuzziness I meant was anytime I was around him, and I could definitely do with some of his firmness. Stupidity engaged, I gestured to the cabin behind me. "Do you want to come in?"

His gaze flicked to the door, and if I didn't know any better, I would have sworn panic flashed across his features. Like a deer caught in the headlights, an image that almost made me giggle.

Liam was far from a deer. He was a predator, moving with the grace and speed of a wolf even on two legs. Dominance radiated off of him in waves. He was both ruggedly handsome and so fucking hot. He was powerful and terrifying.

Lethal and violent.

He adjusted his crotch through his jeans, but there was no hiding that sizable package. "Ah, no. Pack duties, I'm afraid."

Disappointment squeezed my stomach into a painful knot, but I forced a smile. "Sure. I'll see you later."

Before I did something even more stupid like strip naked and throw myself at him, I spun and pushed through the door, shutting it quickly behind me.

After changing into pajamas, I headed to bed and tried to take care of the incessant throb between my legs. It didn't take long to orgasm, but I was nowhere near satisfied.

I tossed and turned for hours, my skin too warm and the pillow too flat. I punched the offending pillow in frustration as if that would somehow fix the problem.

Spoiler alert: it didn't.

At some point Mallory returned home, and judging by the number of stomping clumsy footsteps, she wasn't alone.

Well, good for her.

When the laughs and moans finally ceased, I sighed and gave up on sleep. I slipped out the door leading to the back porch and stood beneath the moonlight, basking in her radiance.

I hadn't used my magic in a few days, not since Amanda's threat, but I itched now to do something, *anything*. Except I couldn't risk getting caught. Mallory had almost walked in on me the last time, which was way too close for comfort.

My gaze flicked to the half-moon, whose energy seeped into my skin. More than enough for something simple like dream-walking.

I closed my eyes and breathed deeply, letting go of my surroundings until I sensed only the moon. My eagerness to use magic fueled the transition, and my consciousness slipped into the dreamscape seamlessly, leaving my body behind.

I knew it was risky with Amanda lurking around, but the slightest touch would rip my consciousness back into place. I could always pretend I was sleepwalking.

The world around me shifted and changed, filling with dense fog before morphing into a new landscape. Darkened trees grew tall around me, much like the ones I'd just left.

Except here, someone had built a funeral pyre in the middle of a clearing, though it had yet to be lit. A man and woman lay on top, their hands clasped over their chests, forever at peace in the sleep of death.

Approaching them, I drew my eyebrows together and examined their faces. Both were older, in their fifties or so judging by human years. I didn't recognize either of them, yet they seemed familiar somehow.

"What are you doing here?" a deep voice growled behind me.

I whirled around with a gasp.

Liam stared at me through narrowed eyes. Wild, dangerous emotions wafted off him like a deadly pheromone. He stepped closer on light feet until we stood toe-to-toe, his tantalizing presence drawing me in and drowning out rational thought.

All rational thoughts except one.

In the dreamscape, he shouldn't be able to see, hear, or touch me.

I should have been invisible.

CHAPTER 15

Rose

My chest rose and fell beneath his intense stare, and my lungs burned with each breath. I was such an idiot.

Of course I'd end up in his dream. How or why he could see me was beyond my expertise, but I was sure it had something to do with my overwhelming attraction to him.

"Where are we?" I asked.

His confused gaze roved over my face before he took a step back, and sadness clung to his hunched shoulders like a shroud. "My parents' funeral."

My heart clenched, and I examined the two faces again. The resemblance was clear now. He had his father's strong jaw and rugged handsomeness, but his mother's nose and full lips. They had been much too young to die.

I'd learned from Mallory that his parents had died about a year ago like mine, which was when he became the pack alpha. She wasn't willing to tell me what happened, saying it was his story to tell when he was ready.

"What happened?" I asked softly.

He moved closer to me, his arm brushing against mine. Electricity zapped through my body, and I bit my lip to silence a moan.

"A misinterpretation." His expression grew dark and shuttered, and literal storm clouds grew overhead. Thunder boomed so loud it rattled my bones, and a bolt of lightning pierced the sky, illuminating the sharp angles of his face.

I wasn't sure what he meant by that, but it was clear he blamed himself for something. "I'm so sorry. I lost my parents, too."

To him, this was only a dream. Keeping up my faux amnesia didn't matter here.

"My father received a prophecy and accidentally killed my mother." His shoulders drooped, and he sighed. "Then we found out the whole fucking thing had been wrong. He succumbed to his grief and rage. I was the only one strong enough to stop him, but he refused to submit. He wanted to die."

Liam clenched his fists at his sides. "I lost them both on the same day."

Oh, goddess, what a terrible thing to experience and burden to endure. It was obvious he blamed himself for his father's death, but it sounded like he had no other choice. I slipped my hand into his and squeezed.

Before I could ask more about the prophecy that caused it all, he faced me, his blue irises darkening beneath furrowed brows. His free hand cupped my cheek, and I leaned into his touch with a sigh.

"Why are you here?" he asked, stroking my skin with his thumb.

The landscape blurred and morphed, transporting us outside Liam's cabin, where I had fought Amanda in wolf form. Where he had trapped me against the rough logs, caught within his massive frame and presence.

Confused at the transition, I met his gaze, and my breath hitched in my throat at what I saw.

Desire, hunger, frustration.

Fear.

Why would he be afraid?

"Because you needed me," I said.

The answer was as simple as that. I could influence where I wanted to go within the dreamscape, but I often let my consciousness drift until someone called out, needing help. I was so attuned to him in the waking world, I must have sensed his underlying pain.

Smoldering lust combusted within his gaze. Gripping the back of my neck, he leaned down and crushed his mouth to mine.

His kiss struck like lightning to my core. An inferno erupted within me, blazing heat incinerating every nerve, every fiber until it sizzled between my thighs. His tongue pressed against my lips, and I opened my mouth, moaning as our tongues touched and danced together.

I was lost in that kiss, falling deep into a sea of desire and need, swept away by inexplicable thoughts of destiny. Everything about this moment felt right, like it was always meant to be.

Fated, and there was no turning back.

Lifting onto my tiptoes, I wrapped my arms around his neck, molding my body against his. His body was hot to the touch, flooding me with unbelievable warmth. His hard muscles rolled across my breasts as he enveloped me in his arms, holding me tight against him.

He groaned into my mouth, his erection pressing into my belly, then slid his hands down to cup my ass. As he lifted me off the ground, I wrapped my legs around his waist. His stiff length teased me through my thin pajama bottoms, becoming sweet, magnificent torture.

A second later, my back hit the grass and his weight settled on top of me. Dew soaked through my pajamas but it was the last thing I cared about.

He broke the kiss and jerked his head back, his face wild with unquenched need. "Fuck. You taste amazing."

With one hand, he ripped the tank top from my body and tossed it away. His hungry gaze took in my bare breasts as my chest heaved with breathlessness. A low, deep rumble built in his throat.

The sound hummed between us, vibrating against the most sensitive place between my legs. I rocked my hips into him, rubbing against the massive length hidden inside his jeans.

Whatever was happening between us, I welcomed it. I wanted more of him, needed him in a way I'd never needed anything.

He dipped his head to my chest, kissing and licking his way across my breasts. Moaning again, I ground against him harder, demanding some relief from the pressure building within.

Moving his body slightly to the side, he slid his hand under the bands of my pajamas and underwear and slipped between my legs. His fingers stroked my slick lips.

I gripped his shoulders, squirming from the tease. He chuckled, and his warm breath tickled my budded nipples. Before I could smack some sense into him, he thrust two fingers inside me and drew my nipple into his warm mouth.

I gasped. The overwhelming sensations increased as he stroked and rubbed and sucked, stimulating me just right. I writhed and whimpered beneath his administration.

"Come for me," he murmured against my chest.

My panting and moaning grew louder as he worked me into a frenzy until I dug my nails into his skin and shattered into a million pieces. My back arched, and I thrust my chest upward, my body clenching around his fingers.

Claiming him as mine.

Oh, goddess. No man had ever worked me the way he just did, and I didn't think it was due to the dreamscape.

No, I had wanted and dreamed of this moment for days, weeks. For forever, it seemed. But it wasn't enough. I still wanted more of him, needed him like I was drowning and he was the air at the surface.

When I finally stopped shuddering enough to open my eyes, I inhaled sharply. Unrelenting desire swam within his gaze.

He lowered his head to my ear, brushing his cheek against mine, and growled, "My turn."

Liam removed his fingers from inside me and flipped me onto my stomach so fast, I let out a yelp. Goosebumps spread across my skin as the cool dew kissed my fevered skin.

After quickly stripping me of my pajama bottoms and underwear, he ran his hands up my legs to my hips. Gripping them tight, he pulled back until I was on my hands and knees, grass sticking to my skin. Air rushed over my naked sex and hardened my nipples once again.

I heard his zipper, then Liam's hands were back on my body and gripping my hips tight, the way I'd dreamed about him doing too many times to count. Growling, he nudged my legs apart with his knee. His erection skimmed my opening, and I whimpered with need.

He nudged his hips forward, parting my lips, then thrust his massive shaft into my wetness, burying himself deep within me.

I'd never been with a man as big as he was, and I cried out as he filled and stretched me. Unparalleled pleasure exploded behind my eyelids. I dug my fingers into the wet grass.

"You. Feel. Incredible." He ground out each word between clenched teeth as he throbbed inside me.

He slid out almost all the way before slamming back into me, his skin slapping against mine and stretching me further. Again and again, he drove in hard and deep until I was moaning and panting from the friction, rocking against him, begging for more.

Harder, faster, deeper.

I wanted it all, all of *him*.

"More," I panted.

His growl strengthened, vibrating between us. My body tightened, throbbing, and my muscles shook with each powerful thrust until...

"Oh, Liam!" I screamed out as my body clenched around him.

Heat infused my limbs, and euphoria flushed through me. Every nerve burst, every part of my being lost in absolute ecstasy.

His grip tightened even more, bruising my hips. He thrust hard twice more before bellowing out my name and releasing inside me. He collapsed over my back, holding me upright with his arms as my body turned to jelly.

Too soon, he pulled out, and I hated the distance, the absence of him inside me.

He scooped me up and held me tight against him, his heart beating loudly against my ear on his chest. His lips pressed against my forehead gently.

Mine.

The word whispered around us, but I didn't know if it came from him, or me.

I was safe, content, and so warm curled up in his arms. For the first time in my life, I drifted to sleep in the dreamscape.

With a ragged gasp, I wrenched my eyes open. I'd dug my nails into the porch's railing, splintering the wood beneath them. My skin practically sizzled from the internal heat as the lingering pulses of my last orgasm faded, and my fast breaths puffed like clouds into the cool night air.

Holy goddess above.

Nothing like that had ever happened before.

And I mean *nothing*.

Not even remotely close. I'd never heard of something like that happening, either. His seeing me shouldn't have been possible, let alone touch me and...

I returned to my bed smiling and closed my heavy eyelids, feeling satisfied for the first time in far too long and already longing for more.

Part Two

CHAPTER 16
Liam

Three weeks of wet dreams featuring Rose had left me more satisfied than I'd been in a long time. Almost every night since she had first appeared in my nighttime fantasies, I'd dreamed of her, envisioned and acted out all the ways I would ravage her welcoming body.

Each night, she would beg for my cock, and I gave her everything she desired. I pounded into her tight, wet warmth until she screamed my name and I came deep inside her.

Against all logic, I roused each morning content instead of sexually frustrated, as if I were actually releasing inside her for the last three weeks. Impossible, of course, but the dreams had been a huge relief and kept my wolf from doing anything irrational.

It's only irrational to you two-legs, my wolf said with an obvious eye roll. *Claiming one's mate is as rational as it gets in the wolf world.*

Chuckling, I stretched out in my bed. Somehow I hadn't managed to come all over the sheets, yet I still woke relaxed and satisfied. Whatever was happening, it had started at the right time.

Only one more night to go until the full moon. One more

night until I could claim Rose for real, and spend every day and night afterward exploring her delicious curves.

Luna help me, I was an addict.

After the first nighttime experience, I had remembered the silver necklace. I'd returned to the location near the falls where we'd found her, wanting to retrieve the necklace as a gift. Perhaps it would trigger a memory, no matter how small.

Only some nesting animal must have beaten me to the punch. It was a disappointment, but I was sure I could figure out something else that would make her smile.

Pack emotions, mainly excitement and agitation, filtered into my consciousness. Frowning, I rolled out of bed and threw on nearby sweatpants and a clean t-shirt before heading downstairs. The house was empty, no Cecilia this morning.

I opened the door and came face-to-face with a fist about to knock.

"What's happening?" I asked.

Caleb grinned. "A witch has been scented. Only a few miles from here."

My heart beat faster. Finally, we had a chance to get some answers. "Gather the hunters."

Releasing an excited whoop, he ran off to do my bidding, and I loped toward the communal hall where we would assemble. A small crowd had already gathered, and excitement buzzed in the air. The intensity grew as I approached.

By now, everyone knew Rose's story, that a coven of witches had held her captive and chased her into our woods when she escaped. Over the last month, most of the pack had embraced her like one of our own, and after tomorrow night, she would be.

I had no doubt she would accept my offer to stay permanently, even if her memories returned. With luck—or torture, if necessary—we would convince the witches to undo whatever curse they'd placed on her.

The light floral scent of moonflowers drifted beneath my nose, and I turned to face Rose. Even now, my heart leaped at the sight of her, and my wolf howled in our thoughts.

I wanted to run my hands through her thick black hair, grip it in my fist while I kissed her without mercy. I would tighten my hold as she knelt at my feet and lifted those big grey eyes, watching me as she took me between her full pink lips. My dick jerked in my pants.

If only she knew the thoughts that ran through my head every time she was near, and just as often when she wasn't. From the arousing scent that always melted off her body when she was around me, I knew she would welcome my advances.

Talking dirty like we did in my dreams might even turn her on more. I couldn't wait to find out.

"What's going on?" she asked. Beneath furrowed brows, her gaze flicked around the gathered crowd.

"I've called for a hunt."

She met my gaze with a curious expression. "Again? Why?"

Our pack had hunted last night, but that was to replenish our storage rooms with fresh meat.

"A witch is on our lands," I said.

Her eyes widened, and her lips parted as she sucked in a breath. It was such a sexy look, and my sweats tightened even more as my erection strained against the fabric.

One more night.

"Let me come," she said.

Oh, she would come alright. Just, not on the hunt. I shook my head. "You know the rules. Only pack members can attend a hunt."

Plus, we didn't know yet whether the witch was alone, and I refused to put Rose in danger. It could be a set-up or a trap. Until we knew why they wanted Rose, why they were willing to risk their lives by coming onto our lands in search of her, I would keep her far away from them.

Her eyebrows drew together tight in a fierce frown. "This

involves me. I'm only here because of those witches. Because of what they did to me."

My jaw cracked as I clenched my teeth. I didn't need a reminder of what they did or might have done to Rose. They would pay for their crimes.

"Even more of a reason for you not to come. It could be a trap." I glanced over to the group of gathered hunters. They were ready.

As I strode toward them, Rose grabbed my arm, and my skin warmed and tingled beneath her touch, as it always did.

"Wait. I need to go," she pleaded. "I need to find out what happened."

I hated hearing her beg—about this, anyway—knowing how unlike her it was. But I couldn't bend the rules for a non-pack member and expect to remain alpha for long. Challenges would follow soon after.

"No," I said firmly. "We'll bring whoever we capture back here." Meeting her determined gaze, I lifted her hand from my arm and kissed her knuckles. "You'll get your answers today."

I left her there, though I sensed her immediate anger and frustration, mixed with a hint of fear. My lips curled into a smirk.

My little white wolf must have been afraid I'd get hurt.

The group of hunters quieted as I joined them. "When we find the witch, my wolf and I will confront it first. If it's truly alone, surround it quickly but stay in the shadows. If the witch doesn't attack, I'll shift to confuse and distract it. Amanda and Bernard, be prepared to secure it quickly."

Amanda's blue-eyed gaze lit with excitement, and Bernard nodded.

"Caleb, bring an ATV," I said to my beta, then clapped my hands together. "No time to waste. Let's go."

Shouts of joy erupted around me, both from the hunters as well as those crowded around. A hunt was always a cause for celebration, but today was different. We had a witch to hunt, and this time, it wasn't to chase off our lands but to get answers for the pain they'd caused one of our own.

I tugged off my shirt and pants as my bones snapped and bent. Black fur exploded across my skin. Mixed with the other clothes, the fabrics fluttered in the air like streamers as we raced on four paws into the woods.

The sun was hidden behind patchy clouds, casting long shadows through the dense trees. Humans would find our prey's trail difficult to follow, but as wolves, we flew over the ground, our steps sure and light.

Miles passed in mere minutes, and the witch's scent grew stronger as we closed the distance. Adrenaline fueled our limbs, giving us the speed we would need to capture the witch before it had a chance to escape again.

When the scent became almost overwhelming, signaling our proximity, my wolf and I leaped over a fallen log and burst through the undergrowth.

A young female witch with brown skin and dark hair stood between two trees. A bandana held her natural afro back from her face, and she wore hiking boots, jeans, a sweatshirt, and a backpack slung over her shoulder. Her eyebrows furrowed as she glanced around her surroundings. She hadn't even noticed us yet.

Such easy prey, my wolf laughed. *Shame they don't trespass more often.*

My wolf and I lowered our head and growled, the hair on our neck rising.

The witch whirled around, and her dark brown eyes opened wide behind thick-lensed glasses. Fear wafted off her body, teasing us. My wolf loved when our prey was scared.

As she whirled around to flee, the other wolves stepped out of the shadows until we had her surrounded and boxed in.

She threw her hands up and scrunched her eyes closed. "Please don't eat me!"

My wolf snarled at her ignorance. Witches were the last thing we'd stick in our mouths. For food, anyway. We would break their bones and shred their flesh with pleasure.

I shifted back to two legs, gaining a sick delight from her grimaces and tightly closed eyes as my body contorted and reshaped audibly. Keeping with our plan, Amanda and Bernard shifted as well, ready to bind her.

When the witch opened her eyes and focused on me again, her mouth dropped open. Her gaze drifted across and down my body. "Oh my…"

Had she been a human, I would have laughed at her reaction. "You're trespassing, *witch*."

She jumped at the sound of my voice, jostling her glasses askew. She pushed them back up her nose and gulped. "I'm sorry, really, I didn't mean to. But I'm looking for my friend. Maybe you've seen her? Black hair and super white skin like a ghost. Kind of hard to miss actually. She's confused and lost, and to be honest, so am I."

Her words poured out in a breathless rush.

I narrowed my eyes, and a growl rumbled from my throat. She'd described Rose perfectly. "Clever story, but I don't buy it. Rose describes her experience with your kind very differently."

The witch's eyes widened again. "She's with you? Oh, my goddess, I was starting to think the worst." She slapped a hand over her heart and exhaled, then glanced around. "Is she here? Is she okay? Can I see her?"

"Oh you'll see her," I said, my voice low and dark. "To answer for your coven's crimes against her."

The witch's jaw dropped open just as Amanda covered her mouth with a cloth soaked in chloroform. The girl gasped and grabbed at Amanda's hand in a futile attempt to get free. A second later, the witch's eyes rolled up, and she slumped to the ground, out cold.

The roar of an ATV's engine cut through the trees, and Caleb drove into sight with a grin. "Easy catch. Just the way I like 'em."

Amanda rolled her eyes. "You mean it's the only way you can get 'em."

"Eh, potato potahto." Caleb shrugged, unfazed by her taunt. He'd already heard them all.

Bernard lifted the witch and placed her on the ATV's flat grate behind the seat. His bright red hair and matching beard created a playful look that was deceiving.

As one of my most experienced and fearsome hunters, Bernard was anything but playful. He tied down the witch's limbs with rope and gagged her mouth with a cloth.

"I only scented the one," I said sharply, cutting in before Amanda could jab back at Caleb. "Anyone else pick up anything?"

"She's alone," Bernard agreed, his voice low and gruff.

The others nodded.

"Let's get this witch back and chained up," I said and let my wolf loose.

"Race you back." Caleb revved the engine and tore off between the trees.

My wolf and I lifted our snout and howled out our success before giving chase.

Soon, we would have all the answers we needed.

And I would have my mate.

CHAPTER 17

Rose

As soon as the hunting wolves disappeared into the forest, the rest of the crowd dispersed, leaving me alone with my terrified thoughts. If they caught a witch from my coven, then my secret would be revealed.

Not that it mattered too much at this point—I was out of time.

The full moon was tomorrow night, and without my charm, I wouldn't be able to cast the spell to camouflage my essence from them again. I'd spent days combing the woods where they'd found me and always came back empty-handed.

Avoiding Liam's questions about why I went there had become more difficult the longer it took. I was sure he wouldn't accept my lame answers about hoping something would trigger my memories much longer.

But after tomorrow, I wouldn't be a witch hiding in a wolf's skin anymore. I would just be a witch, which meant I needed to get far away from here. Unless by some miracle my necklace turned up, and I had really, *really* hoped that it would.

Where had that damn charm gone?

More importantly, why did I want to stay?

If I was honest with myself, I knew why I wanted to stay, but then what? I'd get a new charm and fake being a wolf for the rest of my life? That wasn't going to happen.

I clenched my fists and spun on my heel, heading for the garden. Some of my best thinking happened while I worked.

Thankfully, there were only a few pack members out working the fields and soil. I waved to Cecilia, who was busy humming and clipping spinach leaves into a basket.

As usual, the old woman eyed me as I passed but didn't say a word. Liam had sworn up and down that she was friendly, but for some reason, she hadn't warmed up to me yet. She wasn't mean or rude, just quiet and observant.

The small prickle of fear that always accompanied her presence wormed its way up my throat and clenched. I had a feeling she sensed something off about me.

I didn't know much about her seer ability and whether it allowed her to see the truth of who I was, but it was even more of a reason to get the hell out of here. Before she figured out my secret, or before she blabbed if she had figured it out already.

The fear of the unknown was slowly driving me insane.

I knelt beside my favorite raised planter and dug my hands into the soil. The cool, moist dirt and familiar whispers from the plants soothed my wound-up nerves, and I let out a sigh. Memories rose unbidden, too fast to stop, and my body warmed beneath the onslaught of images and sensations.

How Liam's lips had pressed against mine, and how his hands had run over my bare skin, igniting me with his every touch night after night. How he had felt when he thrust deep inside me until I came undone again and again.

Against my better judgment—for three freaking weeks—I'd visited Liam's dreams almost every night, and somehow each time was better than the last. I was an addict, obsessed even. I couldn't seem to get enough of him, like he belonged to me somehow.

Suppressing a shudder, I shook my head and banished those thoughts. I was being ridiculous.

He was hot, no doubt about it, and an alpha to the core. But he was also surprisingly generous and kind, gentle with the cubs. I was caught off guard each time he was vulnerable around me.

That was all it was. I was attracted to a good-looking man who made my lady bits tingle.

That was the end of it.

Of course I couldn't stay here, no matter how much my heart raged against the idea of leaving and confused the hell out of me. I wasn't one of them. Tears pricked the corners of my eyes, but I refused to let them fall.

No, I wasn't a wolf—I was their enemy.

He wouldn't hesitate to kill me if he knew the truth. I couldn't return to the witches yet either, but I had vowed to make them see the truth about Josef and set them free.

Unfortunately, I didn't know who else I could trust. For now, I was on my own.

"How did I know you'd be out here?" Mal's exasperated voice interrupted my dark thoughts. She was headed my way but still blocked from view by the rows of greenery.

I swiped my arm across my forehead before sweat dripped into my eyes. A glance up at the sun confirmed I'd been out here for longer than I realized, lost in my conflicted thoughts. The spell that would keep my fair skin from burning was one of the few good things I learned from the retreat.

"Yeah, I needed to keep busy."

Carrying a shovel, she stopped beside me and looked over my plants with an appreciative expression. "Nice work. They're flourishing under your care."

I shook the loose dirt off my hands and stood, my stiff muscles groaning. "They would have gotten there eventually. I just gave them a little love boost."

She shot me a skeptical look and leaned against her shovel. "Only you would refer to gardening as a love boost."

Little did she know, this was the only safe place to practice my magic. Other than the dreamscape, that is. But the plants appreciated my help, and I was happy to give it. I liked feeling useful.

Shrugging, I tried to smile. "Gardening feels right. I must have done it before."

Mallory examined my face. "I can tell you're anxious about the hunt."

I really needed to work on my poker face around her. She was far too observant, uncannily so. Like Cecilia. "Wouldn't you be?"

"Maybe, but I'd try to focus on the positive. Come help me." She tilted her head, and I followed her between the rows of planters.

"What's the positive?" I asked as we walked.

"Your memories, duh." She shot me a confused look. "If we catch one of the witches responsible, we can force them to remove the spell. Or whatever they did to you."

She wiggled the fingers of her free hand at me like she was casting a spell, and I couldn't help my grin. No witch in her right mind would cast a spell so sloppily.

Mallory stopped beside a collection of wilting bushes with browning leaves and gestured to them. "We need to get these guys out of here before that disease spreads."

Frowning, I knelt next to one and examined the yellowing spots on the leaves. It was southern blight, but it was a disease that preferred the warmth of the south. I didn't think it occurred this far into the cooler northern forests. "I can treat this."

Her eyebrows shot up. "With what? We've tried everything."

Obviously, I couldn't tell her with magic. I stood and brushed my hair back from my face. "I'm not sure, but it's worth a shot. These are good plants. Give me till tomorrow."

She hesitated, but a commotion back at the hall drew our

attention. Howls drifted through the woods, and an engine revved not far in the distance. Goosebumps rose along my arms.

The hunters had returned.

Mallory and I exchanged a look—hers hopeful and mine wary—and ran toward the front of the hall.

Everyone else must have had the same thought because a large group had gathered by the time we arrived, cheering and shouting in celebration. Caleb had parked his ATV on the dirt road, and Bernard was busy untying someone on the back.

The witch's dark brown eyes were wide and rolling with fear. Her mouth was bound and gagged, and her wrists and ankles were tied together.

Instantly, I recognized her, and my legs wobbled.

Oh goddess...

They'd captured Keysha, my ex-best friend. We'd grown up on the same block and roamed the streets of Washington, D.C. together. As the only other witch I was allowed to be around, she was my closest friend.

Until she, along with all the others, had betrayed me.

I wasn't sure if I was more scared or angry to see her here.

After releasing the last knot, Bernard knocked Keysha off the ATV. With a muffled scream, she fell onto the dirt hard on her side, and her breath whooshed out of her nose.

I clenched my fists at my sides as my instinct to stop them from hurting her kicked in. The last thing I wanted was to see someone get hurt no matter who it was, but my sympathy only went so far. She had believed Josef over me.

She'd brought this on herself.

With her hands and feet still bound, Keysha struggled to her knees, and her gaze jumped over the unfamiliar faces until she landed on mine. Our gazes locked and a spark of recognition flared to life in her eyes.

My mouth ran dry, and I shook my head with the slightest twitch, willing her to understand. To keep her mouth shut.

I'm a wolf. Nothing but a wolf with her pack. No witchiness here, folks. I repeated the ridiculous mantra in my head as if doing so would make it real.

Liam's massive, muscular, *naked* form strode into view, each muscle flexing and pulling taut as he controlled the movements like the fierce predator he was. Beneath a curtain of dark blond hair, his blue eyes were as deadly as his expression. He was so much more vibrant outside the dreamscape.

He was beautiful and terrifying, born and bred to kill.

An alpha above all others.

A shiver ran up my spine. He was a living nightmare, a fact that should have sent me screaming and running in the opposite direction.

Instead, I clenched my thighs together as a desperate need for him built, and I licked my suddenly dry lips.

He was all wolf, and so damn sexy.

Liam ripped the gag from Keysha's mouth. "Tell me again who you're looking for."

Her mouth and cheeks were red from the tight binding, and tears spilled down her cheeks.

A lump formed in my throat.

Could I stand by while they treated her this way? A woman I'd once considered my closest friend?

Yes, she had betrayed me, had even hunted me down through the woods. But I didn't want to be like Josef or the others. I *wasn't* like them. I was better than that, and deep down, I knew Keysha was, too.

"A member of my coven," she stammered out and licked her lips. "Our leader... He was wrong about her. I know that now, but she doesn't need to run anymore. She's safe with us. Safe with me."

Her gaze flicked to mine again, and I held my breath, hoping no one saw or understood her look. She was telling me she was on my side.

But she was also making it super obvious.

I inhaled through my nose, trying to calm my racing pulse. No one here would know she meant me. I'd been a captive wolf, not a witch. She was just looking around, and I happened to look at the same time.

That was all.

Liam's deep voice coiled around my heart and squeezed. "Safe is not how Rose described her experience."

Gasps and murmurs rolled through the crowd.

Well, fuck.

CHAPTER 18

Liam

The witch's scent was thick with fear and disgust, overwhelming any other smells. Still, I knew Rose was agitated. I could sense her thoughts as if she were one of my pack.

My mate wanted answers, and so did I.

"No, that's not the story we heard," Amanda said as she approached the witch and me. Her golden tan deepened beneath the sunlight, and she placed her hands on her naked hips as she stared down the witch. "The new wolf says you and your coven held her against her will. Then you erased her memories before she escaped. *Allegedly.*"

Caleb and Bernard stepped toward Amanda, their eyes narrowed and fists clenched. Her obvious accusation against Rose's story rankled those who had gotten to know Rose the most over the last few weeks.

My growl rumbled loudly in the following silence. "Amanda, stand down. This isn't the time or place for your grievances."

"Of course, alpha." She shrugged and crossed her arms. "My bad."

Whatever misplaced jealousy she harbored for Rose would end today, or I would end it for her. Tomorrow night, I would claim

Rose as my mate, and I would not tolerate Amanda's insolence and disrespect toward her or anyone else again.

I returned my attention to the witch, who watched us with wide eyes. "Do you deny what she said? Are you claiming that Rose lied to us?"

There was no doubt in my mind that Rose's story was true, that she was hunted through the woods by the coven. We had tracked down the witches before they teleported, then discovered her bruised and broken body not far from where they'd been.

This witch would be a fool to pretend otherwise.

"Um." Her chin trembled, and her gaze flicked toward Rose. "I don't know anything about that."

Withholding a sigh, I nodded to Bernard. He hauled the witch to her feet and dragged her toward the treeline.

A cage large enough to hold a standing adult hung suspended from a branch. Right now, it stood on the ground with its door open, but a simple pulley would raise it above our heads.

I'd hoped she would come clean without needing any additional encouragement. Torturing information out of someone—especially a young woman unlucky enough to be born a witch—wasn't something I enjoyed, but these were desperate times.

This witch would be screaming the answers by morning. They all did after a night alone in our woods.

Some of my wolves took it upon themselves to scare prisoners shitless. We didn't have prisoners often, which meant those who enjoyed the game would be raring to play.

A spicy moonflower scent invaded my senses, and I found Rose at my side.

"What are you doing?" Her intense stare never left the witch as Bernard closed the cage's door and locked her inside.

"What needs to be done," I replied. "She'll tell us everything we need to know by the morning."

Rose fixed her narrowed gaze on me. "This isn't right. You can't just cage people like they're animals. You need to let her out."

The rope grew taut, and the witch yelped and clung to the bars as the cage lifted into the air. Her eyes were opened wide, and her knuckles grew white the higher she went.

"Interesting choice of words." I crossed my arms. "You know better than anyone that witches have treated us like animals for centuries. As lesser than. It's time to give them a taste of their own medicine."

The natural pink tint of her cheeks darkened, and her next words were so quiet, I almost missed them. "So you wolves are no better than they are?"

Before I could respond, she whirled and stalked away, her hair flowing out behind her like a black silk curtain. Her lingering scent was full of anger and frustration, but sadness gripped her consciousness.

I snapped my mouth shut and watched her go beneath furrowed brows, confused by her reaction. Surely she must hate witches as much as I did, if not more for the way they treated her.

Why was she defending this one?

I glanced up at the witch, who stared after Rose with wide, fearful eyes as the cage stopped beneath the branch and swayed slightly. Unease prickled across my scalp.

What secret was Rose hiding?

Was the witch in on it?

Aware of Caleb's approach, I shook off the unsettled feeling and focused.

"What was that about?" he asked, glancing after Rose's departing back. She headed in the direction of his sister Mallory's house.

I blew out a breath. "Fuck if I know."

His sharp gaze snapped to me. "You need to handle it. Quickly. Everyone could sense her anger and your lack of response, and Amanda is having a field day with it."

I glanced over to where Amanda stood with a small group. Her grin was borderline malicious as she spoke quietly to them. Whatever she said, the others agreed.

Groaning, I ran a hand over my face. "Send Amanda on patrol. I'll be back in a minute."

"Sure you will," his voice laughed behind me as I jogged down the path leading to Mallory's.

Her house wasn't far, but I'd expected to catch up to Rose before she made it all the way. Instead, she stomped up the porch steps and glared at me from just inside the door. Then she slammed it in my face.

Anger rose hard and fast, as did my hard-on. Clenching my fist, I punched the door, sending it and splinters flying inward. The door flew back several feet before thudding against the hardwood floors with an echoing clatter.

Letting out a yelp, Rose jumped toward the couch with her arms over her head. She stared wide-eyed at the door, then at me. "Are you out of your goddess-damn mind?"

I strode toward her until I loomed over her, demanding obedience as the alpha. Her moonflower scent wrapped around me, tantalizing and mouthwatering. Intoxicating.

Images from my dreams filled my vision and threatened to consume me, her naked body writhing beneath mine and moaning my name.

She straightened her back and lifted her chin, glaring at me.

Clenching and unclenching my fists, I fought to restrain my anger and desire, both competing for the upper hand. My chest heaved. "You disrespected me in front of my pack. I will not allow that again."

One perfectly shaped eyebrow arched upward. "Or else what?"

Oh, hell no.

With a growl, I picked her up and threw her backward onto the couch. Her eyes and mouth opened with surprise, and a hint of excitement flashed across her face.

Before she could recover, I seized her legs and flipped her onto her stomach. Gripping the top of her leggings, I all but ripped them down to her knees, revealing her round, bare ass. Drinking in the unbelievable sight for only a moment, I raised a hand and brought it down hard across her right butt cheek.

She gasped and grasped at the pillow she'd landed on. A bright red handprint marked her skin, but she made no attempt to get away.

I slapped her left cheek just as hard, her ass quivering and clenching beneath the force. Her whimper of pleasure nearly did me in, and I perilously clung to the last ounce of my control.

Until she tilted that beautiful ass into the air. Her scent was fully aroused and begging for more.

Growling, I ran a light hand over the red marks on her skin and squeezed her ass tight. She pushed back against me, encouraging me to continue.

My wolf went wild, demanding release.

Time to claim my mate, full moon be damned. With my other hand, I reached for my pants to push them down.

"Uh, hey, sorry to interrupt..."

My growl deepened, threatening Caleb if he dared to continue that statement or step foot inside this house. I blocked Rose from his view, but there was no hiding the thick scent of arousal curling through the air.

Behind me, he cleared his throat. "It's, uh, you-know-who. We've got a problem."

I closed my eyes and ground my teeth hard enough to be heard. Reining in my wolf was proving to be quite the challenge. He didn't care what was happening with the other pack. He wanted to claim our mate—*now*.

When I finally wrestled him into submission and regained control of my own dark desires, I removed my hand from her ass. She sank onto the couch, covering her head with a pillow.

Considering her bare ass was still on display, it was a cute picture, but my heart clenched painfully when the reality of the situation crashed down.

I'd just embarrassed her. Humiliated my mate.

And for what? My ego?

Her earlier words of chastisement haunted me, that wolves were no better than witches. No better than animals.

Was she right?

Worse, had I reminded her of the trauma she'd escaped?

"Tell Mal I'll fix her door." I turned and strode out the broken frame, knocking into Caleb's shoulder as I brushed past him on the porch. I wasn't angry with him for interfering, but my raging hard-on and absolute lack of control still muddled my thoughts and vision, giving everything a fuzzy edge.

Gulping in the fresh air to clear my head, I aimed for the compound's gate, our usual meeting point. Branches and thorns scratched at my skin, but I didn't care. The minor amount of pain felt like too small of a punishment for how I'd treated Rose.

I clenched my fists. Once I regained control of myself and dealt with whatever Sergio had to report, I would apologize to her in earnest.

I'd always wondered when my father's quick temper would manifest in me. Apparently, I'd just needed to face my mate's feisty nature.

Even now, my dick twitched and hardened again as I remembered the fire in her steely gaze when she challenged me, the way her perfect ass had looked tilted up and ready to receive me. Submissive for the first time, and only because she wanted me as much as I did her.

After a month of flirting yet abstaining, the strong, spicy scent of her arousal had overpowered my will.

"Wait up, man," Caleb panted as he trotted to catch up to me. "I didn't mean to cock block you back there, but he said it was S.O.S. level urgent."

I shook my head as I shoved aside a branch and ducked under.

"I'm glad you showed up when you did. I let my control slip. She deserves better than that."

As my best friend and beta, Caleb knew more about me than anyone. He knew my fear that I would turn into my father, the man who'd beaten me senseless more times than I could remember, all in the name of "toughening me up."

Caleb always believed in me, even when I didn't. He patted my shoulder, and we walked the rest of the way in silence.

My father might have been hard on me, but there wasn't a day that went by that I didn't miss the bastard.

Between a gap in the trees, the gate and Sergio appeared. He glanced around as we approached, nervous in a way he'd never been.

"Things are a-brewin'," he said as soon as we were close enough to shake hands. "Adrian's meeting with other packs nearby, forming new alliances—fast. I'm pretty sure he means to attack after the full moon."

Dread settled across my shoulders, weighing me down. I knew it was only a matter of time before the Howlers' alpha made a move. "You're sure he'll wait?"

The full moon run was sacred to wolves, but that didn't mean Adrian would honor it. He'd done worse before.

Sergio nodded. "He's not meeting with the Bloodmoon Pack until the day after the full moon. He won't do anything until he's secured that alliance."

Caleb and I exchanged a glance.

"Guess it's down to your mate then," Caleb said. "If she's your fated mate, claim her and pray she unites rather than destroys."

I hated that the joy of finding my mate was overshadowed by this damned prophecy...

...and the impending war.

CHAPTER 19

Rose

I closed my eyes and collapsed against the couch cushions, my breaths deep and ragged. Lifting my hips, I tugged my underwear and leggings back over my butt, wincing as the fabric scraped across my raw skin.

Groaning, I rubbed my face with my hands. I couldn't believe I had just gotten wildly turned on by a *spanking*. A spanking for disobedience, mind you, not a playful slap in the middle of sex. At least, not yet.

I wasn't a kinky-sex-type of a girl. Not usually, anyway.

Well, not that I knew of. I had never enjoyed any roughness before now.

Before Liam.

"What. The. Fuck." Mallory's voice carried through the opening that was a door only a few minutes ago just before her shocked face appeared. She stepped through the splintered frame carrying a fabric grocery bag, her eyes wide as she took in the damage and spotted the actual door several feet away.

I rolled off the couch and stood, glad I'd taken a moment to pull up my pants. "I'm so sorry. Liam said he'll fix it."

Her gaze examined me from head to foot, and her shock faded. A smirk played across her lips. "Oh, Liam was here? Is that why you're all hot and bothered?"

My cheeks blazed with heat. I wasn't embarrassed that I found him attractive as a man. Literally anyone alive would. But if she only knew what she'd almost walked in on...

Oh, goddess.

Caleb had walked in.

I couldn't contain it—I laughed. I laughed so hard tears came to my eyes, and Mallory stepped closer with a concerned look on her face.

Waving away her concern, I took deep breaths until I could speak. "Let's just say your brother got quite the eyeful."

Her eyes nearly popped out of her head. "You guys did it? On my *couch*?" Her voice rose several octaves.

"No! No," I said again more firmly, holding up my hands. I grimaced. "Well, almost. But we didn't. So that's good, right?"

She eyed the door again and grinned. "Girlfriend, you made him mad. Like, legit seeing red, raging bull, about to snap, kind of mad."

Make that two of us.

I put my hands on my hips. "He said I disrespected him in front of his pack, but I don't agree with the way he's treating K... the witch." Biting my lip, I hoped she didn't notice my near slip-up. "She was terrified, and technically, he doesn't know if she's done anything wrong. Other than being a witch, I mean."

Mallory shook her head and headed for the kitchen counter. "She knew better than to trespass on pack lands." She set the grocery bag down and started taking things out.

"So the punishment for trespassing is to be caged?" I asked, unable to keep the disgust from my voice.

She opened the fridge, tucking butter and fresh vegetables into drawers. "She belongs to the coven that held a wolf captive and stole her memories. She's just as guilty as the rest of them."

I leaned against the back of the couch and folded my arms. "Has it always been this way?"

"What way?"

"Hating witches like this."

When she finished putting the last item away, Mallory folded the fabric bag and placed it on the counter, eyeing me as she did. "It goes both ways. You don't remember that story either?"

"I'm not sure I ever knew." That was the truth, too. All I knew was that we hated each other, and before now, I'd been okay with my blissful ignorance.

Leaning forward, she rested her forearms on the tiny square island and clasped her hands. "The story changes over time depending on who tells it, but Cecilia's version never does. She claims that when we were still allies a few centuries ago, a wolf and a witch fell in love."

My eyebrows shot toward my hairline. I'd never heard of our kinds being allies, let alone having romantic feelings toward one another.

"They claimed they were fated mates, something that had never happened before. Not between the two species, and certainly not between an alpha and a coven leader," she explained, her intense gaze holding me captive.

"But another witch claimed it was fake, that the witch had deceived the wolf with her magic. He spread horrible rumors throughout the packs and covens. Believing the lies, the alpha wolf rejected his mate, which was also something that had never happened before."

I frowned, confused. "Why would the wolf believe the lies?"

Mallory shrugged and stood straight. "Magic. The other witch who'd spread the rumors cast an enchantment that made everyone believe him, doing exactly what he accused the other witch of." She opened the fridge and grabbed two cans of beer.

"So that one event caused this huge, centuries-long rift?" I asked, incredulous.

"Not quite."

After she tossed one of the beers to me, we popped open the tabs and took long drinks. The flavor had a citrus undertone that I liked, and the crisp cool liquid soothed the fire still simmering inside me after Liam's visit.

Mal stared at her can and continued, "The witch was so devastated, she killed herself. But in doing so, the truth was revealed. The wolf went crazy, rightfully so, and destroyed the entire coven in his grief and rage. Tore them apart one by one. There's been hatred between us ever since."

Whoa.

The story sang like truth deep within my bones, and I couldn't help but wonder about my ridiculously powerful connection to Liam. Since the moment we met, I had known there was something different between us, something deeper.

Luna was known to work in mysterious ways, but she never did anything without purpose. I just didn't know what good could come from my intense attraction to a wolf, especially in this lifetime.

Maybe Luna's purpose wasn't for good, but to drive a wedge further between our kinds. Except, as the mother goddess to witches and wolves, that thought didn't sit right with me. It just didn't make sense.

There had to be more to it.

I gulped down more of my beer, not quite sure what to say yet. Not quite sure I wouldn't blurt out the truth about who I was.

"Depressing, right?" Chuckling, she shook her head. "Anyway, I'm glad you're here. As in here with the pack, and as my roomie. Things have been really good since you arrived. You've added some spice to our lives, and I don't just mean your scent."

It wasn't the first time a wolf had commented on the spicy notes I exuded. Liam's scent, that delicious fir reminding me of Christmas trees, tickled my senses every time he was near, but I was sure it was even more amazing to a true wolf's nose. My spell only changed me so much.

As she raised her can in a toast, her smirk turned devious. "Liam's certainly been happy."

Smiling, I returned the toast before taking a sip, appreciating her comments more than I could say. "It's been a good month, but I'm sure I've overstayed my welcome."

"The full moon run is tomorrow night," she said, fiddling with her can's tab. "We often get new pack members during the event. You could join us if you wanted."

And there was the conundrum.

Going against everything I'd learned growing up, I wanted to stay, and that kind of blew my mind. Over the past month, I'd grown to care for several of the pack members as friends, and in Mallory's case, a bit like family. They were feelings I'd expected to have with my coven.

Unfortunately, I never did, and now I knew my kind had it all wrong. Wolves weren't the problem—witches were. Especially ones like Josef, who sounded a lot like the selfish witch who'd spread the hateful rumors centuries ago.

The problem with staying was the full moon.

My spell would fail tomorrow night without my necklace, which meant I had no choice. I had to leave, at least until I was able to locate or create another highly illegal camouflaging charm without a dime to my name.

Mind you, the spell was only illegal and forbidden because of this damn feud that never should have happened.

In a perfect world, I could have told Liam who I truly was, and he would let me stay anyway. I never would've had to hide the truth if such a tragic end hadn't occurred centuries ago.

With precedence opening the door to possibility, we would have been free to explore this intense attraction without question.

Maybe Liam and I could still have a future together. If we were fated mates...

Nope.

That kind of wishful thinking would get me nowhere.

"We'll see." I downed the last of my beer and chucked it into the open recycling bin.

She made a face at me before her gaze flicked to something over my shoulder. "Oh good, you've come to fix my door."

A dizzying heat spread through my body, and I gripped the back of the couch.

He'd come back.

Even with the distance between us, Liam's deep chuckle rumbled through me, igniting my core. "Not yet. I need to..." He cleared his throat. "I'd like to speak with Rose, if she'll let me."

Hearing my name on his lips made everything tingly again. Taking a steadying breath, I turned to face him. Only, I would never be prepared for the sight of him.

He was everything a man should be and then some. His presence filled the room and devoured the air, stealing my breath until I was almost gasping, begging to be satisfied.

His striking blue irises pierced through to my soul, and a spark of desire lit within them. "Will you walk with me?"

I nodded, not trusting myself to speak just yet.

Mallory's grin turned wicked. "Just don't break down anyone else's doors."

He stepped to the side, allowing me to exit first. The warmth of his hand pressed against my lower back as he led me down the path toward the main village area.

We strolled like that for a few seconds, or maybe a minute. Hell, it might have been an hour for all I knew.

I was lost in the nearness of him, in his overwhelming presence. He invaded my senses, teasing me into a frenzy until I wanted nothing more than for him to take me right then and there, against a tree or a rock or even the dirt for all I cared.

"I owe you an apology." The seriousness of his low voice took me by surprise, shaking me free from the clutches of desire. His hand dropped away from my back, and a shiver ran up my spine from the sudden chill left behind. "I would never want to embarrass or hurt you, and you have my word that an encounter like before will never happen again."

"Not even if I say please?" The words were out of my mouth before I could stop them.

Geez, Rose, you're practically begging for it.

His face snapped toward me, his eyes widening. Then his pupils constricted with desire, and his subsequent arousal pressed against his sweatpants. He ran a hand over his face and groaned. "You're torturing me, you know that?"

I bit my lip to contain my grin. He had no idea I knew about his dreams, that every night we came together—in more ways than one. "I don't know what you mean, *alpha*."

In the blink of an eye, he had me pinned against a tree, his arms boxing me in and the rough bark scraping against my skin. I gasped as his hard length rubbed at the apex between my thighs, and I dug my nails into the trunk behind me just as I had done during one of our nightly forays.

My body throbbed with need as I remembered what had come next.

"You are nothing but trouble," he growled as he dipped his mouth to my neck.

His lips brushed against my collarbone, igniting every nerve of my body in simultaneous combustion. He licked and nibbled his way up my neck and across my chin.

Fiercely and possessively, his mouth claimed mine.

Kissing him outside the dreamscape felt like discovering heaven, like knowing I was safe and loved and happy for the rest of my days.

As his tongue slid over my lips and dipped between, I let out a soft moan. He tasted like moonlight and magic, and our tongues met and danced together with a familiarity that shouldn't have been possible.

I was lost to my senses, consumed by his smell and taste. Seduced by the feel of his rigid body pressed against mine and under my roaming hands.

Our kiss turned desperate and ravenous, needing to be connected in every possible way. The most intimate way. I wanted him harder and deeper inside me.

Biting his bottom lip, I slipped my hands beneath his shirt, dragging my nails up the hard planes and ridges of his abs and pecs. I'd only dreamed of touching him this way, and the reality was infinitely more amazing than any dream, no matter how vivid.

He growled into my mouth, grinding his arousal against me once more before jerking his head back and taking a step away. Each of his breaths was ragged and shaky.

Panting just as heavily, I drew my eyebrows together, confused by his reaction.

"Not yet, not this way." His hungry gaze dipped to my lips, and I was sure mine were as swollen and red as his. "Not the first time."

Flushing beneath his gaze, I clenched my thighs together against the incessant throb. "Are you sure?" I rubbed my hand over the rock-hard length straining against his sweatpants. "I'm not a delicate flower, Liam. This Rose has thorns."

Groaning, he pressed his forehead against mine, his eyes closed. "No. Yes. Maybe. I need a distraction. What can I do to make my behavior up to you?"

I gripped his erection in my palm as he pulsed with the need to release. "This might work."

He snapped his eyes open and pure, unbridled lust raged within his sky-blue gaze. His lips crashed against mine again, and absolute bliss overtook me.

I wrapped my arms around his neck, molding myself against

his body. This man was my destiny, fated to be mine by the goddess above, whatever her purpose might be.

As his arms enveloped me, one hand slid up my back to my head. His fingers dug into my hair, holding me to him, not that I had any plans of escaping.

Of leaving.

And with that thought, the spell of the moment was broken.

Untangling myself, I shoved away from him, gulping in the fresh air. "No, you're right. Not like this."

After adjusting his pants, he ran a hand through his tousled blond hair. His feral grin made me regret my decision. "Then what can I do? For now?"

I took a deep breath, my heartbeat still thumping wildly. "Let the witch go."

Watching for his reaction, I was surprised to see his surprised gaze turn thoughtful. I'd expected apprehension or anger, even lethal outrage.

"Why?"

"Because this feud between our kinds will never end until someone's strong enough to say enough is enough," I said, believing each word down to my soul. "To end the cycle of hate."

He watched me for a few silent moments that sent my pulse racing. Slowly, he nodded. "Okay."

I blinked at him. Once again, I'd expected a different response. For him to argue more.

Was he messing with me?

He took my hands and interlaced our fingers before kissing them. "I'm not sure letting her go will stop the cycle of hate, but if it's that important to you, I will."

Swallowing hard, my desire and willpower to leave him were crumbling. But I had no other options.

While the pack howled and ran beneath the full moon tomorrow night, I would slip away. I knew from my conversations with Mallory that they would all be too busy to notice anything else, even Liam.

I was going to devastate this man, rip out his heart and smash it into a thousand pieces.

The wolves weren't the villains of this tale...

...I was.

CHAPTER 20

Liam

After promising Rose I'd release the witch, I left before I succumbed to her irresistible curves and headed back to the common grounds.

You better make it up to me, my wolf growled.

I did not doubt that I would, many times over. Cracking the tension out of my neck, I strode toward the cage suspended in the air. The sun was playing peek-a-boo behind the clouds this afternoon, and the slight scent of a building storm drifted on the breeze.

Leaning against a tree, Amanda crunched on a half-eaten apple core. The cage's rope was tied to a stake at her feet.

"Let her down," I said, nodding to the rope.

Amanda waved the apple at me as she chewed. "After I finish this."

A growl erupted from my throat. Her disobedience grated on my nerves. "I gave you an order."

"Fine." She rolled her eyes and tossed the remaining apple into the foliage behind her. After untying the rope, she stepped back and released it.

The witch screamed and clutched at the bars as the cage

crashed to the ground. It landed with a rattling thud and sent the witch sprawling across the metal floor. The sounds drew the attention of pack members passing by.

Snarling, I loomed over Amanda. "You know that's not what I meant."

She glared up at me. "Who cares if she got knocked around? She's a witch, or have you forgotten?"

"You are this close to banishment," I ground out between clenched teeth. "Do not test me."

Her eyes widened, displaying a hint of fear. "You wouldn't."

I stepped back and pointed at the whimpering witch. "You will drive her to the edge of our territory and release her."

Amanda's jaw dropped open. "Are you fucking serious? You're letting her go?"

"If I can't trust you with this simple task, you'll be gone by sunset. Have I made myself clear enough for you?"

As I turned around to walk away, Amanda caught my shoulder, and I reacted out of instinct. I grabbed her arm and threw her over my shoulder and onto the ground. I pinned her to the dirt, my forearm digging into her throat.

Her eyes watered from the pressure, but she managed a glare. "At least tell me why you're letting her go."

"My mate reminded me that we are not the savages they like to pretend we are," I said.

Amanda's face drained of color. "Your what?"

Shit.

Releasing her, I stood and stepped back as she got to her feet. I hadn't planned on saying anything until tomorrow night.

"There's something off about her, Liam." She coughed and rubbed her neck. "If you won't find out what the fuck she's hiding, I will."

"Continue that line of thinking, and I won't wait till sunset," I growled.

She stared back at me, disdain and disappointment thick in her scent and consciousness. Without another word, she spun around and ripped open the cage door, snapping the lock in half. She dragged the surprised witch out and away, heading for the pack's garage.

Bernard stepped up to my side, answering my mental summons.

"Follow them and make sure she doesn't hurt the witch," I said.

With a quick nod, my best hunter disappeared into the forest's shadows.

Through narrowed eyes, I watched Amanda drag the witch across the graveled courtyard, hauling the girl roughly back to her feet anytime she tripped and stumbled.

That wolf had gone from one of my best friends and advisors to a bigger fucking problem than I thought.

If only I'd realized it sooner.

THE NEXT NIGHT, THE FULL MOON SHONE BRIGHTLY between dense storm clouds. Luna blessed us with her guiding light for a few moments before the next cloud moved in, darkening the world once again.

Throughout the evening hours, the pack trickled in and gathered around the bonfire. Flames danced and stretched high as if reaching for the moon herself. The earthy scent of charred ash bark mixed with the cool evening breeze, and crickets chirped within the grass and shadows.

I smiled where I stood, my arms folded over my chest. It was time to make my announcement and solidify my future. My gaze found Rose for the hundredth time tonight. *Our* future.

Sitting on a log worn from years of use, she sipped from a cup and stared at the fire. Despite her small smile, she seemed sad, almost melancholy. Someone burst out laughing, and her gaze flicked toward them, a look of loneliness and longing crossing her features.

After tonight, she wouldn't need to feel that way again.

I hadn't understood her request to release the witch and forego answers, but I respected the hell out of her for it. She thought and acted like a natural-born leader, putting others' needs before her own and questioning decisions when they were wrong.

Waking up next to her every morning would be a dream come true. We would figure out a way around the prophecy—together.

Once the entire pack had arrived, I called for silence through our collective pack consciousness. There were a few new faces among the crowd, those who had come from allied packs looking for mates.

One man at the back of the crowd stood out despite the shadows. He stood a head above the rest, possibly closing in on seven feet tall. His facial features weren't visible from this distance, but judging by the way the eligible females eyed him, he was a prime contender for mating tonight.

Good, I thought. We could use his strength in our pack.

As the noise quieted, Rose sat up straight, glancing around warily. The only sounds remaining were from nocturnal animals and insects and the crackling flames.

"Brothers and sisters of the moon, tonight we run beneath Luna's blessed light—"

"But it's cloudy," a young wolf called out before his mother could hush him.

"—even when she's hidden from view." I grinned at the youngster before continuing. "Allow her into your hearts. Let the goddess's will guide you to your future."

My words echoed across the clearing, and a few pack members raised their drinks and grinned or cheered. I waited for them to settle again. "But that's not all. Because tonight, a prophecy will be fulfilled."

A rush of excitement spread through the crowd. Through

rumor and gossip, most had heard of the prophecy I'd received, though only a handful knew the full details.

Standing with the other pack elders, Cecilia smiled knowingly and nodded.

My heart soared with her blessing. Rose had always been nervous around the older woman, even though I'd assured her that Cecilia was only being cautious of a newcomer. She was like a grandmother to me, and her approval of this union freed my lingering concern over the prophecy.

"When I stepped into my role as alpha of this pack, Cecilia had a vision." Walking over to Rose, I took her hand and pulled her to her feet. I looked deep into those wide, stormy grey eyes. "That my fated mate would arrive and unite our warring factions."

Gasps and whispers spilled out around us, but Rose's face had drained of color.

For the first time since making up my mind, doubt about her feelings plagued my thoughts. I shoved them aside, knowing she was likely nervous without her missing memories. We would find a way to regain everything she'd lost.

I could feel the rightness of this decision in every fiber of my being.

"You, my beautiful, thorny Rose, are my fated mate. Run with us tonight, and join our pack." I squeezed her hands and dropped my voice so only she could hear, "Let me claim you beneath the full moon, on a bed of starlight."

A spark lit within my chest, connecting my heart with hers, binding us with a warmth that would last forever.

Solidifying our fated union.

She was mine.

As pack members cheered and howled, her mouth opened and closed without a sound. Confused by her reaction, the doubt lingered in my mind.

"What are we waiting for?" Amanda's voice called out above the din. She pushed through the crowd, and silence fell once again.

Our recent disagreements hadn't been a secret. "Shift, Rose. Kick-off this run as our alpha's chosen mate."

Rose snatched her hands away from mine and backed up, her wide-eyed gaze darting around like a cornered rabbit's.

Amanda's lips curled into a sinister smile. "What's the matter, little pup? Missing something?" She held up her gloved hand and opened her fist. A silver necklace with a blue stone dangled from her fingers.

I frowned. No wonder I hadn't found it when I went back to look. Why hadn't Amanda given it back to her before now?

Gasping, Rose started forward, hand outstretched.

"Uh uh." Amanda clucked her tongue and snagged the necklace back into her glove. Her eyes narrowed at Rose, a dangerous gleam flashing through them. "Thanks to your witch friend, I know your dirty little secret."

Rage exploded through me, and I clenched my fists to keep myself from striking out. But along with the anger came dread.

Something was happening, something bad. Judging by Rose's stricken expression, she knew exactly what Amanda was talking about.

"She's not who or even what she's pretending to be," Amanda said louder, allowing everyone to hear.

The pack rustled with uneasy movements and mutters.

"Amanda..." I warned, my tone promising a harsh punishment if she continued.

"Do you want to tell him, or should I?" She cocked a hip and crossed her arms.

Rose looked between Amanda and me, her scent exuding desperation and panic.

I moved closer, taking her hands again. "Nothing you say will change things."

Amanda barked out a laugh, but I ignored her. I would handle her punishment later. My mate would always come first. We would weather the storm together.

Rose closed her eyes, and a single tear rolled down her pale cheek. "I'm so sorry."

A vise clenched around my heart and squeezed. The prophecy was right, and my worst fears were about to come true.

She would destroy us all.

CHAPTER 21

Rose

Without the charm Amanda found, I couldn't cast the spell allowing me to shapeshift. The full moon had risen and ended that ability. No matter what happened now, midnight would reveal my true essence, fully exposing the truth.

Time had officially run out.

I opened my eyes and gazed at Liam, trying to memorize the lines and sharp angles of his face. He deserved the truth, they all did. Even if it meant giving up my life and destroying his heart.

The bond that had formed between us when he announced me as his fated mate, that golden strand of life connecting us forever, pulsed. A terrible reminder of what was to come and what I had to give up.

He would never accept the real me. Not now. Not after this.

His eyes searched mine, pleading with me to set things straight.

I swallowed hard. "She's right. I'm not who you think I am."

Through our connection, his confusion and hurt filtered through stronger than his emotions ever had before. He drew his eyebrows together. "Okay, what does that mean? Who are you?"

I squeezed his hands, hoping to gain strength from his touch. "I'm sorry that I lied to you. I didn't lose my memories."

Gasps and murmurs of frustration buzzed through the air, but the only thing that mattered was the man standing in front of me. The man whose heart I was about to break, whose life I was about to ruin.

"Oh, come on," Amanda said with an exasperated huff. "Get on it with it already."

My lips trembled, and I dropped my gaze. I'd never been so nervous, so terrified in my entire life. Not even when I ran from the coven. I licked my lips. "I'm…"

"She's a witch."

And just like that, my world shuddered to a stop.

Crumbled.

Frantic, I jerked my gaze up to Liam's face.

His expression had shut down, and no ounce of emotion was revealed except in his gorgeous blue eyes. The depth of pain there nearly ripped my heart from my chest.

He dropped my hands and stepped back, his gaze begging me to say that this was all a sick joke. That it wasn't true.

But it was.

Resigned to my fate, I straightened my shoulders. "I can't lie to you anymore. I won't."

Amanda smirked. "Can't because you don't have your precious gemstone to cast your deceitful spell, you mean."

The lines of Liam's strong jaw moved as he clenched his teeth, and a violent storm brewed behind his eyes. As the spectators' whispers grew louder, hands grabbed my arms from behind, holding me in place.

Not that I had any desire to run.

"Was any of it true?" His harsh tone cut through the rising noise, silencing it.

I winced as someone squeezed my arm harder than necessary. "I ran from my coven, escaped a fate worse than death, not realizing in my panic that I'd entered your territory. They hunted me until I fell, just before your pack arrived, and I cast the spell that hid what I am. It was the only way to survive."

"So it was all a lie." Danger curled around each word like a tightening noose.

"N-no," I stammered, my pulse racing. "What we have, what we feel for each other, what I feel for you is real."

As if helping me, the connection binding us together warmed.

A drizzle fell over the area, mirroring the mood. Liam narrowed his eyes at the ground, his breaths deep and unsteady. Speaking to the respect this pack had for their alpha, no one made a peep.

At long last, he raised his gaze and looked me straight in the eye. All I saw reflected there was darkness.

"I reject you as my mate."

His tone was so emotionless, so matter-of-fact, I didn't register his words.

I refused to.

Until the thread between us pulled tight and snapped. I gasped as a burning pain ripped through my chest, and I threw myself backward. No longer in control of my body, I snarled and bit at the hands gripping me, trying to throw them off.

Trying to get to my mate.

Except...

He wasn't my mate any longer.

Grief crashed over me like a tidal wave, threatening to consume me and devour all of who I was. Blackness seeped into my vision as panic writhed and twisted inside me.

This was wrong. He was mine.

My fated mate.

I knew that now and so did he.

The golden thread binding us dissipated, and my heart and soul splintered apart, shattering into pieces so fine, they'd never fit back together. I sagged against the hands holding me, dropping my exhausted head, breathless.

Lifeless.

"You're banished from our territory. Leave and never return." His voice carried a lethal warning, and his next words cut deep, striking straight through my heart. "Disobey, and I'll kill you myself."

A hush fell over the area as he strode away, the shadows engulfing his massive form until he was gone. My breaths came in shallow gulps, and the world grew hazy.

Someone crouched in front of me, and a rough hand grabbed my chin, forcing me to look up. It would have been painful if I wasn't numb already. My blurred vision focused on Amanda's cruel smile.

"The mating run might be off, but our wolves still want out to play." She shoved my chin away and stood. "Let her go. Tonight, we hunt a witch."

The person holding my arms released me, and I nearly fell forward into the fire before I caught myself on my hands and knees. A single wolf sang to the moon, and uneasy tingles spread across my skin like wildfire.

As the drizzle grew into a steady shower, wolves erupted from pack members' bodies. Snarling and growling, they closed in, surrounding me.

Instinct kicked in, and I scrambled backward, trying to gain purchase on the wet dirt beneath my shoes. My legs trembled as I stood, and I searched through the rain for a friendly face among the remaining pack still in human form.

Many had already left, but those who remained looked away or whispered as they cast furtive glances around the area. Raindrops slid down my face and dripped from my eyelashes and chin.

My lungs seized, making it hard to breathe. I didn't see Mallory or Caleb, not even Cecilia or Bernard. They'd left me to my fate.

I was alone, just like when I arrived.

"Run, little pup," Amanda's voice taunted behind me. "We'll give you a head start."

Despite my heart's desire to lay down and die, I fled into the night. Low, twisted branches grabbed at my arms and hair while vines and slippery roots threatened to trip me. I fell into the mud once, twice, but didn't stop. I couldn't let them catch me.

As I ran, my thoughts cleared. No matter what, I would fight. I would find my way back to my mate and prove myself worthy or smack some sense into him if I had to.

Yes, I had planned to run tonight, sneak away when no one was looking. But that was before he called me his fated mate and solidified the undeniable feeling between us.

It shouldn't matter who our parents were or what they taught us to believe. I would show him what it meant to be a loyal mate. A *true* mate.

A howl pierced the air, startling nesting birds into flight. Two more howls joined in, and my heart leaped into my throat.

I gasped for breath as I ran on two legs. I was faster than a human but certainly not wolves. It was only a matter of time before Amanda and her allies caught up and tore me apart. I ground my teeth.

They could try, anyway.

Tonight was the full moon, when lunar magic—*my* magic—was at its strongest. Even through the thick grey clouds, her power sang within my soul. I would show Amanda that she had messed with the wrong witch.

Snarls and growls closed in as the fastest wolves caught up.

I jumped onto a large protruding rock and launched off, propelling myself over a heap of fallen wet logs. It only took my pursuers a moment to follow, but it was enough time to draw on Luna's power.

Skidding to a stop, I whipped around and threw my arms forward, palms facing the wolves. A moonbeam pierced through the clouds and streamed down, surging into me. Bright white light shot from my open palms and blinded the wolves.

They ducked and covered their faces with their paws, but it was too late. Their vision would be toast for at least a few minutes.

I counted three of them, but more were sure to follow.

Leaving their whimpers of fear and frustration behind me, I dove into the shadows and called them to me. Black wisps curled around my form, cocooning me in their web and hiding me from view as I fled. My steps squelched against the muddy ground, leaving obvious tracks I didn't have time to cover.

Sharp teeth clamped onto my ankle, dragging me down as dazzling pain seared up my leg. I cried out and hit the wet ground hard. The impact forced me to release my cloak of shadows, and my teeth rattled as my shoulder broke the fall.

With my pulse pounding in my ears, I snapped my head toward the light brown wolf attacking me, a wolf I recognized. I slammed my free foot into Amanda's face as hard as I could.

Whining and growling as I kicked her face a second time, she released my ankle and shook her head. Her wet fur flung water and mud everywhere. She refocused her narrowed gaze on me, and wrenched her lips back into a vicious snarl, revealing teeth that could easily shred through my skin, as she'd already proven.

Two more wolves slunk forward. They held their heads low to the ground, and their eyes burned with rage.

The moon's bright light peeked through a break in the clouds, and I drew on Luna's power, weaving together a spell as fast as my fingers could move. I cast the magic, and the light snuffed out, blanketing the area in sudden darkness.

Wolves had better than human eyesight, but that didn't mean they could see in pitch black. They still had supernatural smelling and hearing, however, so I wasn't out of danger yet.

I stood quietly, wincing as I tried to put weight on my injured ankle. Silencing my steps by loosening gravity's hold, I hobbled a few steps away to confuse them if they attacked blindly. The rain would help hide my scent.

The corner of my lips curled upward as a new idea came to mind. Facing my palms down, I loosened gravity across the forest floor and tightened it where I stood, keeping me firmly planted on the ground.

Whines and yelps came from where the wolves had been slinking forward through the dark.

I released my hold on the moon's light, illuminating the area once again. Three soaking-wet wolves floated in the air. Their eyes rolled wildly, and their muddy paws scrabbled at the air as they attempted to gain purchase.

Grinning despite my throbbing ankle, I limped around Amanda until she faced me. "Not such a little pup now, huh?"

Another howl rang out through the woods, not far enough away to be safe.

My time here was up.

I turned, ready to grit my teeth and run on a bum ankle.

Another brown wolf lunged from the shadows, knocking me backward onto my elbows. I sank into the mud, and my hold on gravity slipped. The three suspended wolves crashed to the ground.

The wolf who'd lunged at me bit deep into my forearm. Shooting pains ripped through my arm, and I screamed as my bones snapped beneath the hold. Through blurred vision, I found a moonbeam on the ground a dozen feet away and teleported myself through the prisms of light.

Since I'd once again found myself running without proper preparation, the limited jump was the best I could do. Momentarily free of the wolf, I pushed myself to my knees in the thick mud.

Shivering from more than just my wet clothes clinging to my body, I held my injured arm to my chest as blood oozed down my front. My ankle throbbed beneath me, and I lifted my gaze.

Four wolves stalked toward me, and I knew this was it.

This was the end.

Without advanced preparation, I couldn't take four at once, and certainly not as injured as I was. They would either kill me outright or leave me too injured to heal. Cold rain beat down through the canopies.

Amanda's body bunched as she prepared to lunge.

A massive grey wolf slammed into her side, sending them both rolling through the mud. A smaller grey wolf, though still larger than the others surrounding me, leaped out of the foliage and landed in front of me. She snarled at the other wolves about to attack.

My eyebrows shot up as I fell onto my butt. Someone had come to my rescue. Two someones, but neither one Liam.

Had he realized his mistake and sent the twins to help?

No, he would have come himself if he had changed his mind. They were here on their own to protect me. A tear of relief and gratitude leaked down my cheek.

Hands slid under my armpits, hauling me back toward the safety of the trees, away from the fray. Using my good foot, I helped my rescuer as much as I could, scooting along the slippery ground.

Amanda and Caleb, the bigger grey wolf, attacked each other without mercy, blood splattering across the trees and clumps of wet fur flying. The other three went for Mallory, who spun and bit savagely, holding her own.

The person helping me tugged me behind a wide trunk, and I collapsed against it, panting. Exhausted beyond belief, I rolled my head to thank whoever it was, but the words died in my throat.

Ice filled my veins, weighing me down and freezing my limbs in place.

Oh, goddess, he found me.

Josef.

The man who had charmed me into believing his lies. The coven leader I had run from after discovering his experiments on our fellow witches and friends, stood beside me. The devil I thought I'd escaped.

A self-satisfied smirk pulled up his lips.

I'd once viewed his tall, lithe figure as graceful and ethereal. Until I'd learned how well his slim body hid his sadistic tendencies.

His raven black hair matched equally dark irises, both set against lightly tanned skin. Traits I had once considered beautiful, stoic even.

Except now I knew the truth about what he was—a monster.

Pure evil.

How the hell had he found me out here?

His lips twisted into a cruel smile. "Hello, my sweet Rose. Did you miss me?"

Forgetting my injuries, I tried to scramble away. My broken arm collapsed beneath me, and I cried out as I fell. Wet leaves stuck to my face as I dug my good hand into the muddy soil to pull myself farther away. I'd rather take my chances with the wolves.

Anywhere was better than with him.

His chuckle slithered over my skin, and rising bile burned the back of my throat. "I'd almost think you didn't want me to find you, Rosalind, but that can't possibly be true. After all, you're *mine*."

Getting my knees beneath me, I half-crawled, half-collapsed around the tree.

Still in her wolf form, Amanda crouched on the ground, her head and ears down as she submitted to the beta wolf standing over her, his jaws clamped over her neck. The other wolves had submitted also, and the smaller grey wolf growled to keep them in line.

"Not so fast." Josef grabbed my injured ankle and a charm dangling from his neck, then chanted the teleportation spell that would take us wherever he wished to go.

"No!" I kicked out at him in a frenzy, but he dug his fingers into my wound.

Blinding pain exploded through my foot and leg, and I screamed. My vision went hazy as the agony threatened to take me under.

On my back, I tilted my head and focused on a blurry Caleb, hoping he would realize what was happening in time.

"Help," I whispered.

The big grey wolf released Amanda and fastened his gaze on Josef. A threatening growl rumbled from his throat, and he took a step forward.

Only he was too late.

Josef cast the spell. The world spun and blurred until Luna whisked us out of sight, and everything went black.

Liam

The morning after the bonfire, I awoke in my bed, alone yet again. Cheerful, golden rays of light and chatty birds mocked me through the window.

My chest ached with emptiness, hollow and broken. Even my wolf refused to speak to me, but he didn't understand the seriousness of Rose's betrayal.

Now, she was gone.

I'd rejected my fated mate and banished her from my pack. She might not have united us with our enemies, but the prophecy was fulfilled. Those words would no longer haunt my life, and I should have felt relieved.

Had I not rejected her, she might have torn our pack apart and devastated us for good. Instead, she had only destroyed me.

Once the bond between us had vanished and the pain of the sundering faded, everything had gone numb. Still was, and I wasn't sure I would ever let myself feel again.

I flung the sheets off my body and stormed into the shower, twisting the knob to scalding. I needed to burn her scent off my skin and scrub her presence from my memories.

It was bad enough that she was an actual witch, but her fucked up genetics weren't what ripped out my heart. No, she had lied to me. She hadn't trusted or believed in me enough.

Sure, I might have reacted the same way if she had told me the truth earlier, but she hadn't given me the chance to prove her wrong. To prove everyone wrong.

Instead, I'd had to discover the truth from Amanda, along with the entire pack. She'd given me no other choice.

When every inch of my skin was red and raw from the sizzling heat and intense scouring, I shut off the water and toweled dry. I met my vacant gaze in the foggy mirror.

For the first time in weeks, my dreams had been quiet. No nighttime visit from the woman who'd claimed my heart and soul, only to smash both into a million pieces. No amount of time would heal them completely.

Had she enchanted me through my dreams?

Was our connection ever real?

Or had she used me to get whatever it was she wanted?

Releasing a furious roar, I slammed my fist into my reflection. The glass shattered and sprinkled across the counter and floor, and pain lanced through my hand. Blood dripped down the remaining jagged pieces on the wall and flowed from my knuckles.

A few heaving breaths later, the wounds had sealed, robbing me of the pain I wanted to feel. What I *deserved* to feel.

Whatever. It didn't matter anymore. She was gone. Nothing mattered except the pack, and I could use the distraction of attending to pack business.

At the next full moon, I would choose a replacement mate and be done with this mess. Grinding my teeth together, I tugged on my sweatpants and shirt and flung open the bathroom door.

Caleb and Mallory sat on the end of my bed, discussing something in low, urgent tones. My beta stood with a wary expression, but Mallory folded her arms and glared at me.

"You've made a mistake," she said. "A huge one. Colossal."

I ignored her and headed for the staircase. She grumbled behind me, and the bed creaked.

Caleb caught up midway down the steps, and Mallory's footsteps were hot on his heels. "Seriously, man. She's right."

"No, she's not. My not-as-expected fated mate almost destroyed my pack, and now the prophecy's been fulfilled. It's over. I'm ready to put it behind me and forget she ever existed."

Even as I said the words, I knew they would never be true. I could never forget her.

"That's not all the prophecy had to say," Caleb argued. "It also said she could unite us and—"

Just outside the kitchen, I held up a hand. "That's enough. No witch could ever unite our packs. Let it go."

I pushed open the door with too much force. It banged against the refrigerator and bounced back toward me. Muttering at myself for letting the twins get to me, I stopped it with my hand and entered.

Cecilia's hunched form bustled around the stove, completely unfazed by my loud entrance. The most tantalizing scent of sizzling meat assaulted my nose, and I focused on that. I kissed the top of her grey head before taking a plate and filling it with freshly cooked steak and potatoes.

She harrumphed in my direction as I skirted the island and sat at the kitchen table. Not quite sure what her unusual reaction was about, I raised an eyebrow, but she just clucked her tongue and shuffled toward the sink.

The twins followed me to the table. Caleb leaned forward against the back of a chair across me, and Mallory glared at me again with her hands firmly planted on her hips.

"You're an idiot," she said matter-of-factly.

With my fork halfway to my mouth, I stopped. I lowered the utensil and stared at her. Mallory and I had grown up almost like brother and sister, which meant she got away with more than most.

Still, she had *never* spoken to me like that before, and now, I was her alpha. I wouldn't accept disrespect from Amanda, and certainly not from Mal, either. Once I finished eating, I would call for a pack meeting.

Time to remind everyone who I was—the cold-hearted alpha wolf who'd murdered his own father.

"She's your fated mate, Liam," she snapped. "You don't just throw her away like garbage because she's not a wolf, which the prophecy *clearly* outlined by saying she wasn't what you'd expect."

My wolf grumbled his agreement, the first I'd heard from him since the night before.

I clenched my fork tighter, bending the metal. My patience would not last long. "I did not throw her away. She chose her fate when she lied to me."

"Like no one has ever done that before," she muttered.

Something hard thwapped against the back of my head, making my eyes sting. Letting out a roar, I shoved back my chair. It toppled against the wall where the wood cracked and splintered but remained intact.

A good foot and a half below my six-foot-five frame, Cecilia narrowed her amber eyes and shook her wooden spoon at my face. "I'm disappointed in you, Liam McDonnell. Of all people, I would have thought you'd learned how important interpretation is."

My mouth hung open in shock, her smack forgotten.

"The exact words of my prophecy were she would unite warring *factions*, not packs," she said.

Righting the nearly destroyed chair, I frowned, not understanding her meaning.

She heaved a sigh and shook her head as she shuffled back around the island. "Witches and wolves were not always enemies, you know. We were united once. Strong allies."

"You're saying we're supposed to forgive the witches and

become allies again?" I asked, incredulous. "How would mating one witch end centuries of hatred?"

As she stirred the pot's contents, her stern gaze met mine over the stove. "The rejected witch from ages ago was a lunar witch, a powerful type of magic that rarely manifests and is considered a blessing from Luna herself."

Caleb raised an eyebrow. "How does that help us now?"

"His Rose is also a lunar witch and highly sought after. Hunted like a prize." Cecilia twirled the wooden spoon in the air, sending droplets flying. "Fate has come full circle to right its wrong."

Mallory smacked my arm. "See? I told you. Big mistake. Huge."

"We don't even know if that's her real name," I growled, recalling the rose tattoo on her ankle. Except thinking of her delicate ankle turned into visualizing her long, slender legs, and the delicious scent where they joined together.

Cecilia glanced at me over the rim of her glasses. "It is. Her name is Rosalind Drake."

My mouth dropped open again. Never in my life had I felt this stunned. "She told you her name?"

"No, but not all are as ignorant of the world as you." She turned off the stove's flame, seemingly unaware of or unconcerned with my state of shock. "Josef Weber is also not as good at hiding secrets as he thinks he is."

Recognizing the name, I frowned. The Weber family owned fifty acres of land on our territory's western border.

"You need to bring her back, claim her, and figure out how to heal the rift between us and the witches," Mallory said as if it were the easiest thing in the world to do.

Conflicting emotions surged through me like waves crashing against rocky shores. As prophesied, my fated mate had finally arrived, and I'd thrown her out, just like Mallory said.

Worse—I'd rejected Rose and broken our bond.

Yes, she'd lied to me and betrayed not just my trust but the entire pack's. But I'd let my ego and temper consume and control me, just as my father's had. I'd ignored my wolf and acted selfishly, trying to save face after being blindsided with the truth.

Mallory was right. Rose was far from the first who'd lied to me, and I'd never reacted the way I did last night. I'd overreacted because she was my mate.

Could I blame her for keeping her identity hidden?

She said the coven had hunted her down into my territory. Except she didn't say why she had run or why they hunted her, and I hadn't given her a chance to explain. Instead, I'd acted like a damn fool.

It was time to win my mate back, and I prayed that she would have me again.

"How far did she get?" I growled as I strode toward the front door.

Caleb hurried after me. "Er, bad news on that front."

Dread churned in my gut, and I stopped.

He grimaced. "Amanda riled up a few others to hunt down Rose. When Mal and I found out, we immediately went after them. She was hurt but holding her own. Except..."

A chill crept down my back as I waited for what came next, envisioning the worst. Had I not blocked the pack consciousness from my mind until I could process what had happened, I would have known already.

I could have stopped it.

"Another witch got to her before we could," he said. "He teleported her away."

CHAPTER 23

Liam

My hands shook as fury simmered deep within my chest, ready to boil over at the slightest provocation. A low growl rumbled up my throat.

No one touched my mate but me.

Us, my wolf corrected, breaking his silence at last.

It was bad enough that Amanda had ignored my command and taken it upon herself to attack my mate, even if I'd rejected her. I'd claimed Rose's death for myself, knowing I would never act on that threat.

But now Rose was back with the coven she feared so much she'd chosen to hide among her mortal enemies. Her words last night made my blood freeze within my veins—she had escaped a fate worse than death, and I had forced her back to that fate.

Cecilia's gaze met mine, and the concern gripping her face raised the hairs on my nape. "You'll find her on the Weber estate."

I burst out the front door, calling the entire pack through our collective consciousness. They would heed their alpha's call, especially after last night's drama.

Standing outside the communal hall in the bright morning

sunlight, I waited for every wolf to gather, then I raised my voice to be sure no one missed a word, "As most of you know now, I received a prophecy from the red wolf on the day I became alpha. My fated mate would either unite warring factions or destroy my pack."

Pack members glanced at each other and whispered as I let my words settle in for a moment.

"I thought I'd destroyed us by announcing Rose as my mate before finding out her true identity," I continued. "Not just who, but what she is. I'm here now to tell you I was wrong. We all make mistakes in our lives, and I'm no exception. Last night, I made the worst mistake of my life. I was wrong to reject my fated mate."

Small gasps and murmurs rippled through the pack, and they exchanged uneasy or curious looks.

"The consequences of my poor decision affect us all, and for that, I humbly apologize." I let my gaze drift over the familiar faces, allowing them to see the vulnerability in my expression as well as in my thoughts. "With the threat of war on the horizon, we need allies. Strong allies who can help us secure our lands from those who wish to take it.

"Wolves and witches have been enemies for centuries, and for what? A misunderstanding." I shook my head sadly, remembering the unfortunate ramifications of my father's misunderstanding. "It's time to reunite our kinds. Luna has chosen a witch as my fated mate, and together, we will work to heal the rift that has lasted for far too long between us."

Piercing the stunned silence, a woman laughed.

Through narrowed eyes, I sought the person who found the situation humorous, not at all surprised to find Amanda's face.

She shoved her way to the front of the crowd and stood with her arms folded across her chest. "You've lost your goddamn mind, Liam."

Low growls rumbled through the pack and several took steps

toward her, but I held up my hand to stop them. Unlike this woman, they obeyed their alpha.

"I take it you've got something to say before you leave this pack?" I kept my voice calm and steady despite the rage still simmering deep within.

She'd overstepped for the last time with her stunt last night. Speaking to me this way only solidified her fate.

"You're weak," she snapped, her blue-eyed gaze filled with loathing. "You've lost your backbone to that witch. You don't deserve to be alpha of anyone, let alone this pack."

I barked out a surprised laugh. Female alphas were rare but not unheard of. "Are you challenging me?"

Her smirk chilled me to the bone.

"No, I am," a deep voice said behind me.

A vaguely familiar man lumbered forward, towering over the others' heads, all of whom stepped back with wide eyes to allow him through. He had to be nearly seven feet tall and built like a tank.

His short, dark brown hair matched his brown eyes, and thick black eyebrows cast shadows across his sun-weathered face.

Although he'd stuck to the shadows last night, I remembered him at the bonfire. It wasn't unusual for wolves from other packs to join our runs, searching for a mate as well as a new home.

I'd looked forward to having his strength against the Howlers, but it seemed he had other ideas for joining us.

"And who are you?" I asked, using my alpha presence to calm the others and keep them back. While I appreciated my pack's support, a true alpha challenge was to be respected by all.

Amanda's smug voice cut in, "As of last night, Heath is my mate and a new member of our pack. If you hadn't been sulking all night, you would've met him already."

The man's hard gaze met mine as he cracked his neck. "I challenge you for the alpha title."

Eyeing Heath from head to toe, I knew I could take him. It wouldn't be easy, especially if his wolf form was as imposing as his two-legged one, but he proved his inability to lead a pack with that challenge.

Being alpha wasn't a title. It was a respected role within pack life.

Alphas ensured the pack's safety and sustainability. It wasn't a task for the faint of heart, especially with the Massanutten Howlers nipping at our doorstep.

"Challenge accepted," I said, adrenaline already pumping through my veins.

Fur exploded from both our bodies. Bones snapped and reshaped as our wolves seized control.

My wolf and I shook out our midnight coat and appraised the challenger's wolf. He was nearly all black except around his snout and eyes, where brown showed through.

There was no doubt he was bigger than us, but bigger didn't always mean stronger, or faster.

Or smarter, my wolf added. *This pack is ours.*

We lunged for each other.

Immediately, Heath's wolf went for our throat, but we ducked our head and clamped onto his front leg. Our strong jaw crunched through the bone.

He let out a whine and bit down on our neck, tearing through the fur to reach skin. My wolf and I threw our weight against him, body-checking him and forcing him off balance.

We circled each other with our lips pulled back and saliva dripping to the ground, looking for weaknesses. My wolf and I darted in, biting deep into his flank until we tasted blood, then bounced away.

Swiping at us, he caught our back legs and pulled, knocking us down. He took advantage of our lower position and tackled us as he dove for our neck again. His teeth sank into our skin, ripping through tendons and muscles.

Adrenaline kept the deep wounds' pain from overwhelming logic, but pinned to the ground this way, we couldn't defend ourselves properly. Our heart pounded against our ribs as we felt the first flash of fear.

No, my wolf growled. We *are alpha here, and our mate needs us. Finish this.*

Renewed strength and determination surged through us. We rolled, ignoring the agonizing pain as Heath's teeth tore through our throat before slipping away. Lunging upward, we caught the side of his face and bit down hard. Blood gushed into our mouth.

Without releasing our jaws' hold, my wolf and I raked through his chest and side with our claws. Warmth splashed over our paws, and Heath's whine rose to a wail.

His steps faltered until he collapsed to the ground, and he tucked his tail beneath him in a show of submission.

We released him, and my wolf growled in Heath's nearly destroyed face before allowing our change back to human form.

When I stood on two feet over the wolf's heaving body, I gazed out over the pack. *My* pack. Crimson sweat dripped down my chest and arms. The gash through my throat throbbed with my pulse, but my wounds were already healing.

"Are there any other challengers today?" I asked, infusing my words with the alpha's lashing command.

A few pack members adjusted their weight nervously while others glanced at friends and neighbors. No one else stepped forward, and one by one they knelt and bowed their heads.

This wasn't like kneeling for a king out of pure obligation. It was a sign of respect, acknowledging my dominance and leadership. Had they been in wolf form, they would have done as Heath had and tucked their tails between their legs.

They knelt until Amanda was the only one standing, her fists clenched by her side. She trembled with rage.

I fixed my gaze on her. "You and your mate are banished from this pack. You have ten minutes to retrieve your things and go."

Turning my back on a woman I'd once considered a close friend, I strode toward the open garage with Caleb, Mallory, and Bernard fast on my heels. Inside, I grabbed a bag lying on one of the work tables and pulled out a fresh pair of sweats and a t-shirt.

We always kept extra clothes and supplies on hand, and all vehicles faced out for fast maneuvering.

"I'm not gonna lie, I was a little nervous," Caleb said with a grin as I dressed quickly. "That guy was fuckin' huge, but you put him down *fast*. No one's gonna challenge you after that, brother. Not from this pack."

Bernard tilted his chin down. "Alpha."

"Ass kissing can come later." Mallory twirled her hand impatiently.

"Cal, stay here and keep an eye on the pack." I opened the Jeep's driver's side door. "Make sure Amanda and Heath are gone before we get back, and call Bernard immediately if they try anything shady. Or if anyone else does, for that matter."

Knowing his place as my beta, Caleb nodded and gave a quick salute. "You got it, boss."

Mallory climbed into the Jeep's passenger's side and slammed the door. "I'm coming, too."

I wasn't going to argue. Like all my wolves, she was trained to fight, and we had no idea what we'd face against the coven. I might need the extra set of teeth.

Bernard jumped in the back through the open top, and I slid behind the wheel. I threw the Jeep into gear and slammed my foot down on the gas pedal. The tires squealed as we tore out of the garage and onto the road leading out, and mud flew into the air behind us.

For reasons unknown to me, the coven had terrified Rose. Her fellow witches had hunted her down when she tried to escape. Now, they had her again thanks to my foolish actions.

The only thing Rose had given away was that she escaped a fate worse than death. My pulse raced, throbbing in my neck as I spun the wheel in the direction of the Weber family's lands.

What horrors awaited her back in the coven's clutches?

Was I too late to save her?

CHAPTER 24

Rose

A tickling sensation brushed against my hand, and I groaned as I regained consciousness. I felt like I'd been thrown into a meat grinder or trampled by a herd of horses. Every part of me hurt, and my ankle and arm throbbed in time with my heartbeat.

What was left of my heart, anyway.

Something soft and wet nudged at my fingers. I flinched in surprise, but my arms were bound behind my back, restraining my movements.

I snapped my eyes open. Soft sunlight streamed in from the nearby window, allowing me to see that I lay on my side on a bed. A fluffy white pillow supported my head.

A tiny squeak came from behind me, and a brown mouse climbed up onto my shoulder, peering down at me. His little pink nose wiggled, brushing his whiskers against my skin.

The tight gag kept me from laughing out loud, but I smiled as tears gathered in my eyes. I had missed Mouse dearly. I'd planned to bring him with me when I first ran from Josef, but things hadn't gone according to plan, not even remotely.

I'd found Mouse almost a year ago when I first moved into Josef's house—well, his mansion. His humongous family estate served as the coven's home, and we lived under his roof during training retreats. He'd required it.

Mouse's presence meant I was back in Hell. A brick dropped into my stomach, ruining the reunion's joy.

Evil had found me.

I was doomed.

Mouse squeaked again and scurried down my back, brushing against my fingers. The ropes binding my wrists tugged, and a barely audible gnawing sound reached my ears. He was trying to chew through the rope.

Oh, sweet Luna.

My hope soared through the roof. If he could get me free, I could use my magic to get us the hell out of here.

Lifting my head to take in more of my surroundings, I recognized my old room at the Weber estate immediately. It was hard to forget this place, with furnishings and comforts far nicer than anything I'd had growing up.

A white gauze canopy spread over the four-poster oak bed and pristine white comforter, and a dresser stood against one wall. Two doors led into an ensuite bathroom and out into the second-floor hallway.

The door across from me opened, and Josef stepped in from the hall. My heart sank like a boulder dropped into a fathomless sea.

His raven black hair looked ruffled, and, adding in the sweatpants, casual v-neck shirt, and slippers, I would bet he'd just woken up.

I couldn't believe I'd once found him handsome. All I saw now was a monster.

As I watched him warily, his dark gaze swept over my body and settled on my face. A cruel smile lifted the corners of his lips. "Looks like I have perfect timing."

Exhaustion and the tight rope kept me from sitting up, so I

pulled my arms closer to my back, scooping Mouse into my palm so he could keep working without being seen.

Josef had never discovered Mouse, and I planned on keeping it that way. There was no telling what he would do to the tiny creature.

After closing the door behind him, Josef sat on the edge of the bed. The bedsprings creaked beneath his weight. "Do you know how lucky you are that I found you?"

I glared at him, unable to respond with the gag in my mouth. Not that I wanted to chat with the arrogant asshole. More like scream until his eardrums burst.

His nearly black irises gleamed. "If it hadn't been for Keysha, I may have been too late."

Uncertainty riddled my thoughts. Maybe I was wrong about my friend after all.

Had she betrayed me again?

"After her unfortunate encounter with those dreadful dogs, she knew you were in trouble. She was sure they held you against your will and begged me to help you escape." His smile turned even more sinister. "Now, you're back where you belong. You're safe, and I'll ensure you remain by my side for many years to come."

I closed my eyes, and a single tear slipped down my cheek to the pillow. Not knowing the full extent of his horrifying experiments, Keysha had thought she was helping me. But by involving Josef, she'd destroyed me.

A cold, clammy hand touched my calf.

My eyes flew open, and I jerked my leg away. The movement jostled my injured ankle, and nausea rolled through my stomach. Burning acid shot up my throat, and I groaned through the gag.

I swallowed with difficulty, not quite sure if I'd drown if I threw up while gagged. I didn't want to find out, either, not unless it was my only way out of here.

Death would be far sweeter than a life with him.

Josef's hand hovered above my leg, and he chuckled. "You may be wondering why you haven't healed yet. You see, I'm not sure you understand the gravity of your situation yet. I've stopped your body from healing until you agree to my terms."

I snorted. Like hell I would agree to anything this man offered.

He reached toward my face, and I flinched away. Unfortunately, I couldn't go far while bound. Not without squishing Mouse.

As Josef untied and removed the gag, his fingers brushed across my cheeks. Acid once again burned its way up my esophagus. Only this time it was from his touch and not the pain. I licked my cracked lips and stretched my sore, tingling jaw.

At least now I could vomit without drowning. Maybe I would get lucky and puke all over him.

"Water," I rasped out, my tongue sticking to the roof of my mouth.

Grabbing my arm, he hauled me into a sitting position, then picked up a cup from the bedside table. He brought it to my lips, and his black eyes held a menacing gleam as I tilted my head back and let the sweet relief trickle into my mouth. He pulled the cup away after one tiny sip and returned it to the table.

I looked at it with longing, my thirst far from quenched.

"Submission is such a better look on you." With a smug smile, he leaned back against the bedpost. He crossed one foot over his other leg, clasping his hands around his knee.

So casual, like the arrogant bastard wasn't holding me against my will. "Why are you doing this to me?"

"Because you're meant to be mine, Rose. I understand you were scared by what you saw before you ran, but Luna brought you back to me, proving that I'm right." His tone took on a hard edge, and his knuckles tightened as he gripped his knee. "As my bride, your magic and your body will be at my disposal."

A chill spider-walked down my spine, and my stomach shriveled in on itself. Silently, I urged Mouse to hurry. "That will never happen."

"Oh, but it will. Because failure to submit means I'll have to kill Keysha, and I'll make sure everyone knows that you're to blame."

Another icy wave of fear and revulsion hit me. Keysha and I had grown up together, done everything together, including attending the retreat and joining his coven. It wasn't her fault that things ended up this way.

Now, Josef was threatening to murder an innocent woman and one of my closest friends just to make me do his bidding.

His evil knew no bounds.

"And then what? If I'm blamed, you won't get my magic. I'll be in prison, or executed," I said, stalling to give Mouse more time.

Whatever Josef planned for me after this little pep talk wouldn't be good, and I didn't doubt that whatever he would do to frame me would look real. He was too cunning, which meant I needed to be ready to act.

The magic council overseeing the covens and some of the other supernatural creatures would lock me up at the barest mention of murder. I would have approached them months ago about Josef if I had gotten any solid proof against him.

Josef smiled, making the tiny hairs on the back of my neck stand on end. Rising from the bed, he moved to look out the window, and the light fell across his face. "You have no idea how special you are, do you?"

My eyebrows drew together in confusion. He'd made his attraction to me and my magic more than clear, but this felt like something else.

Unexpected images of Liam's face illuminated by sunlight flooded my thoughts. I inhaled sharply as the gut-wrenching pain of his rejection returned like a punch to my gut.

I wanted a chance to tell him how sorry I was, how wrong I'd been. There were so many things I needed to say and to set right, but there was no point in wallowing in the past. I swallowed the lump forming in my throat.

Hindsight's anchor might drown us all in the end, but only if we let it. I would get free, and then I would worry about Liam.

"Your parents were either smarter than they looked or complete idiots for not telling you," he murmured.

Angry heat flushed across my cheeks, along with threads of guilt that accompanied their faces. My parents had died not long after I left home for the retreat, involved in a horrific car accident.

Our last conversation had ended in an argument about joining Josef's coven after the retreat. I never had a chance to say goodbye, to tell them how sorry I was for not believing them.

Shame joined the guilt clenching my stomach in a vise. My list of regrets was growing far too long.

Josef faced me, his gaze raking over my body in a way that made me want to gouge his eyes out. "Whatever their reason, lunar witches are rarer than you realize. Once in a generation kind of rare, and your magic is more potent than any who have come before you."

I blinked in surprise. Well, that explained why I'd never come across another lunar witch before, but I also didn't have much experience with witches outside of my parents, Keysha's family, and Josef's coven.

My parents had sheltered me from the magical world, claiming it was just how things were done. Different supernatural species didn't mingle, they said, and practicing magic wasn't all it was cracked up to be.

I was only now realizing they might have kept me away for an entirely different reason.

"Why didn't you tell me this before?" I asked.

"And risk losing you to the magic council's greedy little claws?" He scoffed. "No, I couldn't let you or the others know too much. But that's beside the point. Whether you agree to my offer doesn't matter. I will take your magic from you if I have to, though that process will be most unpleasant...for *you*."

Goosebumps crawled across my arms. I knew exactly what process he referred to. Memories of the witches' withering figures would haunt me forever.

One of the ropes loosened, and Mouse's tiny paws moved to my other hand.

Rolling my shoulders as if needing to stretch, I gently shook my wrist free of the rope. I opened and closed my fist behind my back, trying to dispel the tingles as blood rushed back into my hand.

I needed to keep Josef talking.

"So, what? You're just a power-hungry maniac?" I let out a harsh laugh. "Talk about a boring cliché."

His expression darkened, and he took a menacing step away from the window. "My entire life has been filled with people doubting me. Schoolmates ridiculed me for my earth magic, always seen as *lesser than*."

Of all the magical classes, earth magic was viewed as the lowest or least formidable, and fire the highest because of its quick offensive capabilities. Lunar magic wasn't even listed, but I'd never questioned Josef's reasoning, that it was too inconsequential.

I didn't know how my magic compared to the others, but judging by his obsessive interest and vague comments, I would guess high. Possibly even above fire since he hadn't become obsessed with Beverly.

He pressed his fists into the mattress and leaned forward until he was right in my face. His warm, sickly sweet breath swept over my skin. "I will be shunned no longer. I'll have a beautiful woman on my arm and in my bed, your magic at my disposal and at my mercy. Everyone will learn to fear me."

Try as I might not to, I gulped, and his gaze tracked the movement with a malicious smirk.

"I will have my revenge, my dear Rose." His voice was quiet, and he lifted a hand to brush a strand of hair back from my face.

I hardly dared to breathe, afraid my slightest movement would provoke him. The second rope fell to the comforter behind me, and Mouse jumped off my palm. I prayed to Luna that he had run for cover.

Josef's fingers drifted across my cheek until he cupped my chin, his touch turning my stomach in revulsion. "Hearing their screams will be so sweet."

His gaze moved to my lips. "Just like when I killed your parents."

CHAPTER 25

Rose

Everything around me faded away as I struggled to process his words. Josef had killed my parents?

That didn't make any sense. They'd died in a single-car crash. Even without witnesses on the scene, the evidence had been conclusive. I had seen the autopsy report.

"How?" My throat constricted, making it hard to breathe. "*Why?*"

"Oh, it was easy enough for my earth magic to send their car over that bridge's concrete barrier," he said casually, though his grip on my chin tightened. "I warned them to let you go, but they wouldn't listen. I had no choice, you understand. You were always meant to be mine."

A tingling, prickling sensation spread beneath my skin, burning through my veins. It took me a moment to recognize what it was. Rage and grief so deep, so consuming, I wasn't sure I'd ever satisfy the hunger for revenge.

I was hot and cold and charged with so much electricity I thought I would burst. I needed an outlet.

With my arms now freed thanks to Mouse, I tugged on the

moon's magic and lifted my palms. Pure moonlight blazed into Josef's eyes.

Screaming, he raised his hands to ward off the dazzling flare as if it would do him any good.

That was my cue. I rolled off the bed and landed on my feet. Splinters of pain shot up my calf as I put weight on my injured ankle, and I grabbed the bedpost to stay upright.

As much as I wanted to kill him right here and now, I was a mess. I needed help.

Biting my lip hard enough to draw blood, I staggered for the door, letting out a small whimper as I used my bad foot for balance.

Still blinded, Josef spun around and threw himself at the door, blocking the way. He blinked rapidly and sneered. "I see you've gained some new thorns."

As he stretched out his arms and felt through the air, I dropped to my knees. My gaze settled on the heavy metal bedside lamp.

Crawling toward the side table as quietly as possible, I took a deep breath before grabbing the light in my good hand. In one swift move, I stood on one leg and slammed the lamp against the side of his head.

Thank Luna the cord reached.

As his hands flew to the gash in his head, he lost his balance. He staggered sideways, just enough for me to reach the door. I gave his back a push for good measure, sending him sprawling, and hurled open the door.

Unfortunately, I'd used my broken arm.

Clutching my wolf-bitten forearm to my chest, I shuffled across the hallway toward the stairs. Tears streamed down my cheeks as my arm and leg throbbed.

At the top of the floating staircase, I hesitated for a moment, knowing the descent was going to hurt even worse. His thudding steps burst from the room. I had to move.

Each step down had me seeing stars. My legs wobbled, threatening to collapse at any moment, and nausea churned in my stomach.

With the last step in sight, a figure dropped in front of me and landed in a crouch, blocking my escape. I yelped and fell back against the stairs.

Josef's face was a mask of frenzied wrath as he stood.

Voices called out from other halls, echoing across the mansion's polished black floors. New figures dressed in various types of pajamas ran into the foyer to see what the commotion was about.

Coven members I'd lived with for months stared in shock as they recognized me. I was sure I looked like a wild woman still covered in mud and with twigs stuck in my hair. At least some of them still had a wild case of bedhead.

"Attack her!" Josef yelled, pointing at me. "She's lost her damn mind. She's deranged!"

Two of the five witches reacted immediately, twisting their hands in the air and chanting fast.

I called on the moon's energy again and cast a reflective shield just in time. The bluish light reflected their thrown spells, sending their magic ricocheting in other directions. Witches ducked to avoid getting hit. One wasn't so lucky, and she fell to the ground, convulsing and twitching.

Gritting my teeth, I pulled myself to my feet, holding onto the railing for support. "He's lying to you all, as usual. Has no one else wondered where our missing sisters went?"

I looked at each of them, staring them down until they dropped their gazes or glanced nervously at their neighbor. "They're not as missing as you think. Check the hidden basement. That's where I found them."

Suddenly, I couldn't move my arms or legs. Most of my body was frozen in place. I glanced at Josef, expecting an attack. Except he also stood completely still, his eyes rolling wildly with manic fury.

As he opened his mouth to speak, Juliet raised her open palm and uttered a magical command. She closed her hand, and his mouth slammed shut.

Long, flaxen hair hung loose down Juliet's back, rather than up in the severe bun she usually wore during the day. The white hair growing in at her roots wasn't nearly as visible in this style, but her sleeveless pajama top revealed the leathery, aged skin of her arms.

After Josef and me, she might have been the next strongest witch in our coven. She or Beverly, who thankfully hadn't run in with the others.

Juliet's brown eyes focused on me. "Why did you run from us?"

"When I discovered Josef's secret, he held me captive," I said with a shudder, loathing the memories. "I escaped, but he'd turned all of you against me. I had no choice that night but to run."

"If that's true, then you left us to be his next victims?" Disbelief was evident in her tone and raised eyebrows.

I frowned at her insinuation. "I tried to warn you about him, all of you, but no one believed me. Beverly made sure of that. I planned on coming back once I got help."

"Laura, go down to the basement." Juliet grimaced as she continued to hold us with her mind. "And please be quick about it."

Laura's bright blonde hair whirled out like a fan as she sprinted out the front door. She was one of the few who'd been kind after Beverly's smear campaign against me.

My thoughts were muddled from everything that had occurred that night, but a prickling sense of dread crept through my mind. I'd only found the basement by happenstance when he took Constance. No one questioned the basement's existence just now.

The young witch returned a minute later, breathless. Panting, she shook her head at Juliet and cast a glance at me. Behind her glasses, fear tinted her hazel gaze.

Shit.

I glared at Josef. "Where did you move them?"

He widened his dark eyes in a look of innocence that only fools would believe. "I don't know what you're talking about. As I said, she's deranged. She needs help."

"Bind them both until we know the truth," Juliet commanded.

Energy vibrated through the open room as Laura extracted metal particles from the surrounding air and earth. Moving her hands in a complex weave, she shaped and molded them into thick chains and directed them at Josef and me.

A heavy weight settled over and bound my wrists and magic. I winced as the manacles dragged against my wounds, which still weren't healing.

Juliet released her control of our limbs, and I collapsed onto a step.

Whipping around to face Laura, Josef forced a smile and held out his secured wrists. The metal prevented both of us from casting spells. "Remove these now, and all will be forgiven."

"What is the meaning of this?"

Closing my eyes, I groaned. I didn't need to look to know who'd spoken. Beverly's shrill voice was heard far too often in this house.

Several pairs of footsteps followed her into the foyer, and I struggled to lift my heavy eyelids again. Two women flanked my archnemesis—Alicia and Melissa.

Fantastic. She'd brought her entourage of bullies.

Beverly had pinned her chin-length brown hair away from her face, and without makeup, a thick smattering of freckles trailed across her cheeks and nose. Like the others, she and her minions wore pajamas, but Beverly completed her look with fluffy slippers.

Before Juliet had a chance to answer the question, Beverly thrust her palm forward and a fireball zoomed toward Laura.

The novice witch screamed and dove to the side. With her concentration diverted, the chains binding Josef and me dissipated.

His twisted gaze met mine, and he grinned. Raising his unbound arms, he wove a spell into the air. The earth trembled beneath our feet.

Except Josef turned out to be the least of my concerns.

CHAPTER 26

Rose

The front doors burst open and three blurred shapes ran inside. A massive beast with fur the color of midnight leaped into the air and collided with Josef, knocking him to the floor.

Liam.

My heart and soul soared, blazing with triumph. He'd come for me.

Unfortunately, my triumph was short-lived.

The floor heaved. Chunks of black concrete surged upward and slammed into the monstrous wolf, sending him sprawling head over tail. He was back on his paws in a flash and circled Josef, who'd surrounded himself with a wall of swirling concrete, torn from the floor.

The two grey wolves snarled and snapped at the other witches, who huddled together in small groups. They held their arms up, preparing spells to fight back.

My body shook, but it wasn't just from exhaustion or anger—it was also fear. This fight was about to turn into a blood bath.

At the center of the concrete maelstrom, Josef stood and brushed dirt from his pants and shirt. Fury etched harsh lines into his face. "I should have known you mongrels wouldn't be far behind."

Liam growled and charged at the witch. At the last moment, he crouched and sprung upward. His paws cleared the concrete wall's top, and he opened his jaws to seize Josef.

The witch was ready for him. He directed the largest piece of concrete at Liam. The slab knocked the wolf to the side just before his teeth grazed Josef's raised arm.

As Liam tumbled to the floor, the concrete block that was almost as large as he was fell on top of him. He tried to get his legs beneath him, but the concrete held him in place as if an invisible hand pressed from above.

"No!" Fear gripped my heart in an icy cage. I couldn't let this happen. I couldn't let him die. Grabbing the stair's railing, I intended to haul myself up and stop this madness.

Only someone beat me to it.

"Everyone stop!" a familiar voice yelled.

Stepping into view, Keysha drew her hands together and clapped. The eardrum-shattering thunderclap of her magic dropped everyone to their knees.

Along with the other witches, I slapped my hands over my ears, and the grey wolves whined and shook their heads. Josef's swirling concrete barrier crashed to the floor.

Taking advantage of the distraction, Liam scrambled out from under the block. He leaped at Josef and slammed him to the floor with a sickening crack. Saliva dripped onto the witch's face as the black wolf held him beneath his paws, baring his teeth in a vicious snarl.

"She's telling the truth about Josef," Keysha moved to stand beside me, and her kind brown eyes urged me to believe her. She held out her hand to help me stand.

Clutching my broken arm to my chest again, I took her hand and pulled myself up onto my good foot. I glanced down at Josef. "Where are they?"

"Are you hearing yourself right now?" Beverly interrupted, her face contorted with disdain. "Josef's been nothing but kind to you, allowing your sorry orphaned ass to stay here long after he should've kicked you to the curb."

Still in her wolf form, Mallory growled at the witch and inched closer to her legs.

Beverly raised her chin, seemingly unafraid of the threat. "You honestly expect us to believe your pathetic lies that he's obsessed with you?" She scoffed and gestured at me. "Don't fall for this scam, ladies. She's delusional, and apparently, Keysha's more gullible than I thought."

My best friend's face darkened with anger, and she pushed her glasses farther up her nose. "Raise your hand if you've ever witnessed Josef's mask slip."

Tentatively, hands began to raise until almost every witch present acknowledged the truth. The only ones whose arms remained at their sides were Beverly and her followers.

Keysha cast a quick smile at me before glaring at Beverly. "Tell us again how Rose is the delusional one."

Throughout this entire exchange, Josef remained silent on the floor. The black wolf's growls rumbled louder, and he snapped his teeth closer to Josef's face. His claws dug into the witch's chest, blood pooling around each paw.

Josef quivered, but his jaw remained clenched tight.

The audacity of this man in the face of his imminent death turned my vision red. My skin prickled with heat as a burning rage rose within me once again.

This witch had killed my parents, murdered them in cold blood to fulfill his demented fantasy that we were meant to be together. He'd lied to everyone, gaslighting me for months until I finally saw the truth for myself.

My pulse pounded in my ears, my anger building to an inferno until I was about to combust.

No more playing it safe.

I drew on Luna's magic, pulling every ounce of moon magic down into me. My rage demanded justice, and I would give it what it desired.

Blue and white wisps twirled around my body as I harnessed every last drop. The cosmic energy coalesced in my outstretched hand, spinning and crackling with astral lightning.

I wove a spell so massive, I thought I might burst before I finished. I wasn't even sure it would work—I'd never attempted anything like this before. Unfortunately for Josef, I would risk anything right now.

The witches must have sensed the building energy because they took several steps away, their expressions wary.

When my spell was ready, I released a tiny blue thread toward Josef. My magic curled around his neck and tightened like a garrote.

His eyes bugged out of his head, and he writhed on the floor beneath the wolf's giant paws.

"That's only a fraction of the pain you'll feel if I release the entire spell," I warned him. As I held back the remaining magic, sparkling starlight danced around me, lifting my hair as it floated in a celestial gravity. "I will obliterate you, your very essence, even your soul. You'll feel every atom of your being ripped apart, and it will not be quick."

Sizzling energy and a sulphuric scent filled the air.

"Josef." Despite the rage churning inside, my voice was calm. I waited for the bastard to meet my gaze, relishing in the agony showing within his dark eyes. "I won't ask you again. Where are they?"

He gritted his teeth. "Attic."

Juliet nodded to Laura, who eyed the wolves with caution. Mallory growled but let her pass, and she ran past me and up the steps. Only a moment later, Juliet called down for help, and the wolves keeping the witches back stepped away.

Two witches hurried up the stairs to help Laura with whoever was hidden in the attic. I didn't know who, if any, had survived.

Satisfaction and relief settled into my exhausted limbs, and I fell to my knees. I wouldn't be able to hold my spell much longer.

"What was he doing to them?" Juliet asked, kneeling beside me. Her shoulders carried the weight of the world.

I met her gaze with sadness. "Stealing their magic."

She sucked in a sharp breath.

Movement caught my eye across the hall. Beverly held her hand to her mouth, and her face had drained of color. Her lackeys glanced nervously at their leader and the other witches.

I wished I could enjoy that moment and laugh at them for their foolish ignorance. But too much had happened, too many women were hurt by this weak man's selfishness.

Liam let out a bark to get my attention and lowered his wolfish head to Josef's throat. Raising his questioning blue gaze to mine and baring his teeth, his intention was clear.

Still bound by the starlit energy wrapped around his neck, the witch trembled against the broken floor.

I glanced at Juliet, whose jaw set with determination. She nodded.

"Step back," I said to the black wolf and met Josef's terrified gaze. "We won't let you harm anyone else. Your end has come, and I guarantee Luna will not try to save your tainted soul."

For the briefest of moments, Liam hesitated before releasing the witch and obeying my command.

A rueful smile tugged at my lips. The alpha wasn't used to anyone else ordering him around. Well, he better get used to it.

Praying that Liam and the others were far enough away, I cast the remainder of my spell. My back arched painfully as the vast amount of magic I had harnessed released in a rush.

The cosmic energy spun toward Josef like a ravenous vortex and crashed into him. Swirling darkness consumed his body. As his agonized screams rent the air, lights flickered and ceiling debris crumbled to the floor.

A frigid wind rushed through the foyer. Clothes and hair billowed wildly as the gale added to and spun around the sphere of magic.

The spell's magnetic force expanded, tugging everyone and everything toward it, threatening to consume the house itself. Picture frames and art flew off the walls, and chairs in surrounding rooms shrieked as they dragged against the floor.

The black hole's energy swelled even further. Witches cried out and clung to whatever they could. All three wolves dug their claws into the quaking floor, leaning back and away from the magic.

My hair whipped in front of me, and I curled my good arm around the stair's railing. My heart pounded, and I wondered if I'd gone too far.

I met Liam's wolfish gaze across the room. Pouring my love into that moment, I urged him to see the truth on my face before my spell obliterated us all.

The black hole exploded, shooting fireworks outward from its center. I ducked and covered my eyes and face with my arm as a rush of warmth swept over me.

Silence filled the area so suddenly, I thought my eardrums had burst. I hadn't even realized how loud the damn spell had been until it ended.

Or maybe I was dead.

Time to find out.

Slowly lowering my arm, I peeked my eyes open and blinked until the dancing spots in my vision cleared. The last of my magic dissipated into the air, winking out like dying stars.

Josef was gone.

In my opinion, it was far too quick a death for all the pain he'd caused, but it was over. The nightmare had ended.

My eyes rolled into the back of my head, and I collapsed.

CHAPTER 27

Liam

Sitting in a chair beside my bed, I stroked the back of Rose's delicate, smooth hand. She slept peacefully, as she had for the past two days since I brought her back to my cabin.

Cecilia had assured me Rose would awaken, that she had just overexerted her body physically, emotionally, and magically. I had to trust that the old seer was right, but it wasn't easy.

My wolf whined in our thoughts, echoing my fear that Cecilia might have been wrong.

Thanks to her witch genetics, Rose's body had completely healed while she slept. Her broken ankle and forearm had mended, and every inch of her skin was as white as it used to be. Every inch except for her rose tattoo.

Now, we just had to wait for her to open her eyes. To smile at me once again.

I prayed that she would forgive me.

Caleb's peppermint scent preceded his soft knock at the door. "Checking in on you this morning, brother. How's our Rose?"

"Same."

His footsteps approached, and he rested his hand on my shoulder. "She'll pull through. She's way tougher than she looks."

This woman was a rose in every sense of the word. Breathtakingly beautiful and soft to the touch. Yet undeniably fierce and strong. Unbreakable.

I nodded, managing a small smile. "Yes, she is."

Her finger twitched beneath my hand, and I held my breath. My pulse raced as I leaned forward. "Rose?"

Her long dark eyelashes fluttered before her eyes blinked open. She looked around in confusion, drawing her eyebrows together tight. When her gaze landed on Caleb and me, her grey eyes widened.

"Oh, thank Luna." I let out a quick laugh and brought her hand to my lips, then clutched it in both hands. "I thought I'd lost you."

Her storm-colored gaze fell on me, and various emotions churned in my gut.

Caleb squeezed my shoulder. "I'm gonna give you two time to catch up."

A moment later, the door clicked shut.

I reached over and grabbed the cup beside the bed, bringing it to her lips. She sipped the water, never taking her eyes off me, but I couldn't read her expression. My heart pounded.

She had every right to hate me after what I did to her, everything I put her through. But I didn't know what I would do if she couldn't forgive me. If by some miracle she did, I would prove myself worthy of her love every day for the rest of my life.

"I'm sure you have a dozen questions, and I'll answer them all." I set the cup back on the table and took her hand again. "But most importantly, I need to tell you that I'm sorry. I'm sorry for not making you feel safe enough to tell me the truth, and I'm sorry my ill-thought-out actions led to what they did. I would never have forgiven myself if…"

My voice caught, unable to put words to that nightmare.

Rose held up her free hand. "Stop."

My lungs constricted, and I dropped my gaze. It was too late to fix my mistake. I certainly didn't blame her, not after what happened. She probably never wanted to see me again.

"How did you find me?" she asked, her voice hoarse.

Not ready to see the hurt and disappointment I'd caused, I kept my focus on her delicate hand encased in mine. "Cecilia knew who you and Josef were. The Webers' land borders ours."

Silence stretched between us.

"He killed my parents."

My head snapped up in surprise. "What?"

Her haunted gaze met mine. "He found out about me some-how, before the retreat. Found out about my magic and how rare it is. He invented this fantasy that I was destined to be his, my magic and...and my body."

A shudder ran through her, and it took all my strength not to grip her hand tighter. I didn't want to scare her, but at that moment, I wished she hadn't killed Josef.

Because I wanted to rip his fucking head off.

That makes two of us, my wolf growled.

"He murdered them to keep them away from me, to stop them from ruining his plans," she continued, swallowing hard. "They knew the truth. They'd tried to warn me."

A tear rolled down her cheek, and she swiped it away.

My heart felt like it was breaking all over again. It destroyed me to know that anyone had caused her such pain, one I knew all too well. I wanted to wrap her in my arms and never let her feel pain again.

Rose's gaze flicked to our joined hands, and she squeezed mine gently. "If it hadn't been for you, he might have won."

Hope flared to life within me, and I held my breath.

She smirked and met my gaze. "Well, you *and* the twins."

I let out a surprised laugh. Oh thank the heavens, she cracked a joke. Her smile was like the light at the end of a dark tunnel.

She tugged on my hand. The desire flaring to life within her intense grey gaze stiffened my cock. "Come here."

Finally, my wolf howled with excitement.

"I need you, Liam."

Those four words were all it took to break the last shackles of my fear and guilt.

I stood and grabbed the sheet, yanking it from her naked body. As goosebumps spread across her lily-white skin and hardened her pink nipples into mouth-watering nubs, I dragged my gaze across every delicious curve.

All of that was mine.

She was mine.

After stripping off my shirt and pants, I climbed onto the end of the bed and in between those long, slender legs. I had no intention of disobeying her command, but she deserved so much more first. A proper apology.

Starting at her foot, I kissed and nibbled my way up her leg. My cock grew painfully harder with every moan and whimper she released. The tantalizing scent of her arousal curled around me, tempting me to forget everything else and thrust inside her.

To claim her.

She gripped the sheet in her hands as I pushed her thighs wider apart and closed in on her perfect center, the origin of her intoxicating scent.

Meeting her burning gaze, I licked the length of her pink lips and flicked my tongue across her clit. She gasped and bucked her hips against my mouth. She tasted exactly as she had in my dreams —spicy yet floral, like the air during a full moon.

Unable to resist that temptation, I slid her legs over my shoulders and dove into her warmth. I thrust my tongue inside her eagerly and circled her sensitive nub with my thumb.

Her gasps and moans got louder and faster, and she released the sheets to tangle her fingers in my hair. Her grip tightened, holding me against her as her hips rose to meet my mouth.

I chuckled against her skin. Knowing that I was the one giving her this pleasure, this escape from her demons, my cock pulsed, ready to explode. I slipped my tongue out and sucked in her clit.

"Oh, Liam!" Her thighs clamped around my head as her hips bucked off the bed.

I thrust my tongue back inside her while she climaxed, drinking in her sweet nectar as she clenched around me. When she collapsed against the bed panting, I dragged my tongue up her lips, catching every last drop of her pleasure as she shuddered from aftershocks.

My dick ached with need, and I climbed up her body. I stopped to capture her hardened nipples between my lips, sucking on each. Her hands ran up my arms and shoulders, urging me higher even as she whimpered and arched her back, demanding more.

I kissed and licked my way up the salty skin of her neck, then across her chin to her mouth. She moaned as I thrust my tongue between her lips, letting her taste herself on me. She responded eagerly, her tongue meeting mine before sucking my bottom lip into her mouth.

When she bit down on my lip, I couldn't wait any longer.

I propped myself up on one arm and positioned my tip at her slick entrance. Her cheeks were flushed and her eyes bright as she drank in my body above her. I waited until she met my gaze, wanting to see deep within her soul when I finally entered her.

"Claim me," she breathed.

And I did.

With one swift thrust, I was inside her and heaven at the same time. Rose cried out in pleasure, her tight warmth enveloping me until it was all I felt or knew. No dream could compare to this moment.

She wrapped her legs around me, holding me close. "Oh, goddess, Liam, you were made for me."

My name on her lips was driving me wild. I rested my forehead against hers as I slowly withdrew. Our eyes met, and I plunged inside her again, releasing a low growl.

She gasped, and her eyelids fluttered shut.

As I slammed into her again and again, the need to release built. My thrusts deepened, and her hips rose to meet mine, opening for me fully. Her breaths came out faster, and she raked her nails across my back.

This was everything I'd wanted, everything I'd needed since I first laid eyes on this woman. She was my mate, my equal, and I would get to spend every day for the rest of my life inside her, hearing her scream my name in ecstasy.

As I claimed her with each thrust, a new kind of heat radiated between us, weaving the mated bond and uniting us once again.

"You're mine," I growled. "Say it."

"I'm yours, only yours!" Her body clamped around me as she orgasmed again, and she thrust her breasts upward. "Liam!"

My balls tightened, and I bellowed out a roar as I released deep inside her. Her inner warmth pulsed, milking me for everything I had.

When I finally stopped coming, I collapsed on top of her without pulling out. I wanted to stay inside my mate for as long as possible. Breathing heavily, I buried my face against her neck, breathing in her moonflower scent.

Rose's legs slid to my sides, and she draped her arms around me. She tangled her fingers through my hair and drew lazy circles across my back as our panting slowed.

I propped myself up on my forearms and lost myself in her gaze.

She cupped my face in her hands and stroked my cheeks. "And you're mine."

Lowering my head, I kissed her swollen lips gently. She was absolutely right and would be until the end of time. Already, my dick started to harden inside her.

She slid her hands down to my chest and pushed against me

hard. Caught off guard, I rolled sideways, and she followed, straddling my hips.

Her long black hair fell wildly around her in a glorious cascade, and hunger flashed like lightning through her storm-colored eyes. She wasted no time sliding back onto my stiffened length, capturing me inside her sweet warmth.

As she rolled her hips rhythmically, I slid my hands up her thighs and gripped them tightly, earning a deep, lustful moan. I stared up at this magnificent creature who had claimed my heart and soul. She was absolute perfection, a goddess.

Starting today, I would rise to the occasion and fuck her senseless any time she desired.

CHAPTER 28

Rose

S ore in the best way possible, I followed Liam out of his cabin and toward the pack's communal hall. His big hand slipped into mine and squeezed, and my heart just about jumped out of my chest with joy.

We had spent the entire previous day and night wrapped up in each other, hardly coming up for air or food. I was insatiable, and thankfully, so was he.

The morning sun greeted a bright blue sky as we strolled down the path. Birds flew overhead and called out to one another, and a couple of squirrels shook leaves loose as they hopped across branches in a game of chase.

It was the perfect summer day.

Or it would have been if we weren't on our way to face my coven.

After the black hole had consumed Josef and I'd passed out, Liam had scooped me up and ordered the witches to follow him. For reasons I had yet to figure out, all but one had obeyed without complaint.

As we left the forest's shadows and approached the village's enormous hall, pack members waved or cast wary glances in our direction. Liam had told me what happened with Amanda and her mate Heath.

He also told me that he'd chastised the entire pack for hunting me down—or allowing it to happen—without a direct order from their alpha. I felt bad they'd received a tongue-lashing because of a situation involving me, but they also should have known better than to listen to Amanda.

Since I didn't want to start off as the alpha's mate on the wrong foot—er, paw?—I'd chosen not to accept Liam's offer of additional punishment for the wolves who'd chased me down through the woods.

Besides, their friends and family members were giving them a hard enough time as it was.

Unfortunately, I hadn't had a choice in the next matter. Liam led me inside the communal hall and stopped, waiting for the breakfast crowd to notice our arrival.

My preference would have been to sneak up a back staircase with as little notice as possible, but Liam reminded me that it was important for the pack to see me as a strong leader who didn't hide or cower from difficult situations.

I hadn't thought this whole "alpha's mate" thing through thoroughly enough before letting the bastard claim me. Memories of the last twenty-four hours surged, and heat spread through my limbs, collecting between my thighs.

Yeah, it was worth it.

As soon as one wolf spotted me, they all did thanks to their shared pack consciousness. I had no idea whether I'd gained that ability once Liam claimed me, but now seemed like a good time to find out.

Here goes nothing.

I took a deep breath. Envisioning a net cast over the gathered pack, I urged a sense of peace and forgiveness outward from my thoughts.

Judging by the gasps and sounds of surprise, I must have done it right.

Liam snapped his wide-eyed gaze toward me and grinned. "Still full of surprises, aren't you?"

I shrugged and smiled, but my heart filled with warmth as dozens of emotions returned and spun through my mind—appreciation, regret, and even downright giddiness from some of the younger members. The majority were happy to see their alpha choose a worthy mate, no matter my supernatural species.

Of course, there were a noticeable few who refrained from responding via our shared consciousness. I wouldn't worry about it too much, but I made a mental note of those wolves.

Liam gestured me toward a staircase to the second level, and I made my escape. Living among wolves had taken time to adjust to; leading them beside a man like Liam was a whole other endeavor.

At the top of the stairs, a short hallway deposited us into a meeting room with a high, sloped ceiling. The height gave the room an expansive feel, and two skylights provided ample natural light.

A long oval table and a dozen chairs took up the right side of the room while a few more comfortable chairs and couches were scattered around the remaining space. Several Skyline pack guards plus Caleb and Mallory stood beside the table, and six members of my old coven, including Juliet, Laura, and Keysha, sat on two couches speaking quietly.

My best friend for as long as I could remember jumped to her feet and ran toward me as soon as we entered. Her black afro bounced with each step.

Two pack guards cut her off with menacing scowls, and Keysha skidded to a stop with her hands up. "I just want to hug her. I swear!"

Letting out a laugh—or maybe a sob—I rushed toward her and squeezed her tight. A small squeak startled me, and I immediately let her go.

"Someone else missed you too," she said, reaching down the front of her button-up shirt. When she pulled her hand out, she held Mouse. "He came to me a few days after you left. After my initial freakout, I checked the basement, but it was empty. I didn't know what to believe."

I scooped the little brown mouse out of her hand and brought him to my face. His whiskers tickled my cheeks as we greeted each other with a nose rub. This time under much better circumstances.

Warmth pricked at the corners of my eyes. "Oh, I've missed you too, Mouse."

Liam's hand spread across my back as he leaned closer. "So this is the little guy who saved my mate? I owe you a sincere thank you."

Mouse bobbed his head, then scurried up my arm. Reclaiming his favorite perch on my shoulder, he peeked out from beneath my hair.

I smiled at Keysha. "Thank you."

She grasped my hands in hers and squeezed. "You have to know how so, so sorry I am. I should never have doubted you, but Josef was incredibly persuasive. I feel like a total ass."

Goosebumps spread along my arms. I knew exactly how persuasive he could be—no, had been. He was gone for good. "It's in the past, honestly. I want to let it go and move forward."

"That is exactly why we're here." Juliet met my gaze as she approached. "Your mate has shown us kindness and generosity we don't deserve after the way we treated you. The metaphorical blindfold has been removed from our eyes, and we have a proposition for you."

I raised my eyebrows and glanced at Liam. He'd narrowed his eyes at Juliet, but I could tell it was more of a cautious optimism rather than suspicion.

"We've come to the unanimous agreement that you should lead our coven going forward," Juliet continued. As my mouth dropped open, she shifted her gaze to Liam. "Furthermore, we would like to offer our services as ambassadors, championing a reunification between witches and wolves and becoming allies once again.

"Of course, this is assuming you agree with our recommendation, Rosalind."

The other witches nodded and grinned, and Keysha winked.

Surprised didn't even come close to what I felt at that moment. Never in my wildest dreams had I seen this meeting unfolding the way it was now. I was happy—no, more like ecstatic that they supported me enough to become their leader and also wanted to mend the rift between our species.

"You're willing to forget centuries of hatred because of this one experience?" Liam's incredulous tone mirrored my shock.

Juliet chuckled. "We are, yes, but that doesn't mean others will. It will be an uphill climb—"

"A *very* steep climb," Keysha muttered.

"—but I see no reason not to try," Juliet said. "If we've learned one thing from this experience, it's that there are always two sides to every story, and the easiest one to believe is not always the right one."

I thought I would have to give up my coven, perhaps even all covens, after Josef's lies took root. This was an almost unbelievable blessing.

But what would that mean for my life and future with Liam?

Would I have to give one of them up?

"See? You were worried about the prophecy for nothing. She didn't destroy the pack after all." Caleb slung his arms around Liam and me, pulling us close. He tilted his head toward Liam. "*You* almost did, though. Good thing she's one badass witch."

Liam's murderous gaze fastened on his beta.

With a laugh, Caleb let us go. "I'm just sayin' a heartfelt, 'You were right, Cal,' is in order."

Before Liam could inflict bodily harm on his best friend, I

snagged my mate's hands in mine. "What's he talking about? What prophecy?"

As Liam grimaced, Mallory smacked her brother on the arm. To his credit, Caleb managed to look guilty.

"I knew I'd catch you talking about an old wolf behind her back," a woman's strong voice said from behind Liam.

He stepped to the side to let Cecilia hobble her way into our gathering.

As usual, the woman's grey hair was tied back into a slick bun, but her amber eyes were as sharp as ever behind her glasses. She trained her gaze on me. "Once I figured out what you were hiding, it clicked. The factions weren't the packs."

I glanced between her and Liam. "I don't understand."

"You and I shared a similar secret," she said with a wink. "You weren't the only witch hiding amongst the wolves."

My jaw went slack. Nothing could have shocked me more, but I was in good company. Liam's eyes had narrowed to dangerous slits while Caleb's were about to bug out of his head. Mallory and the witches all shared puzzled expressions.

And here I thought she hadn't liked me when in reality she was probably wary of me figuring her secret out.

Before anyone could gather themselves enough to form words, she chuckled. "Nobody hurt themselves thinking about it too hard. Where did you think a wolf seer's magic came from? Luna? Pah."

She shook her head. "Red wolves come from generations of mixed heritage with the witches. The bloodline has thinned since the divide between our kinds and too few seers are born these days. Now, we can fix that."

Liam's crystal blue eyes met mine, which had widened in a look of shock. "When I became the Skyline Pack alpha a year ago, Cecilia had a vision that my fated mate would either destroy our pack or unite warring factions."

My eyebrows shot toward my hairline. That was a hefty

burden to bear for anyone, let alone a man who'd just lost his father and become a leader.

"Why would you take such a risk with me?" I asked.

Liam chuckled and raised my hands to his lips, kissing them softly. "For you, my sweet Rose, I would risk everything."

Keysha snorted, then fell into a coughing fit. She pushed her thick-lensed frames up her nose and waved away Laura's help. "Sorry, it's just... Have you told him why your mom changed your nickname from Lin to Rose?"

I grinned at Liam's confused expression. "She always said she should've known right from the start. She said I was beautiful yet wickedly stubborn and deceived people with my delicate exterior."

"She also called you prickly," Keysha added. "Often."

"I mean, she wasn't wrong, especially when I was a teenager."

Liam brushed a strand of my hair behind my ear, his hand lingering against my cheek. "I look forward to learning everything there is about you, prickly parts and all."

The bond between us warmed and tingled.

WE SPENT THE REST OF THE MORNING SITTING AROUND the table, discussing the idea of ambassadors to reunite our kinds. Six witches were present, and two were still recovering from the horrific siphoning. Two others hadn't been so lucky and had joined Constance in an early grave, succumbing to their bodies' exhaustion.

After we took a break for lunch, I took in the faces of my mate and my friends, and a weight lifted from my heart and shoulders. My life was getting back on track. For the first time in over a year, I felt like I was where I was meant to be.

I wished getting to this point hadn't been such a rocky ride, but I also knew that even the slightest change could have altered this outcome. As much as it pained me to accept Josef's involvement in my parents' death, I never would have met Liam otherwise.

It was a bittersweet thought, but my mother had taught me not to dwell on the past, and I would honor her memory by following her teachings.

A knock against the doorframe drew our attention to the opening. A younger pack member named Damian glanced at us nervously as he hesitated in the doorway.

"Yes?" Liam asked, frowning.

Damian's back straightened beneath his alpha's direct gaze. "It's Amanda and Heath, sir. They've joined with the Massanutten Howlers."

Liam and Caleb exchanged a glance, one that immediately raised goosebumps across my skin.

Our work to establish peace was only beginning.

Will they succeed in their mission to reunite the witches and wolves? Or will this fated union destroy the pack once and for all?

Rose and Liam's journey continues in

————

THE PACK'S FATE
Wild Magic: Lunar Legends Book Two
Coming soon!

————

Need something to keep you busy until it's released?

Join a shapeshifting thief and a grim reaper agent's adventures in

WINGS OF FIRE
The Last Phoenix: Book One

~ *Available now on Amazon* ~

Interested in more? Stephanie shares new release alerts, exclusive giveaways, and her special brand of humor in her bi-monthly newsletter. Sign up here! You can also visit stephaniemirro.com for even more information on each of her books.

Ready to review? Reader reviews help other readers discover new authors and stories they might enjoy. Please take a moment to leave a review for *The Wolf's Secret* on Amazon.

Want to find other readers who love Stephanie's work? Join Stephanie's VIP reader group on Facebook to meet like-minded individuals or chat with the author herself! Visit Mirro's Magical Mortals today!

Feedback: Did you find a grammatical error or have a problem with this ebook? Let Stephanie know at stephanie@stephaniemirro.com

HAPPY READING!

Acknowledgments

As with all my books, I couldn't have done this without the support of my family, friends, and fans.

My husband and mother-in-law are saints for putting up with my scattered brain, which is usually thinking about a gazillion things at once, including worlds and characters that technically don't exist.

I love sharing my overactive imagination with my kiddos, who in turn love making up stories with me, such as The Many Adventures of Eggy and Bread (and their baby Bregg).

My beta readers are the best around, somehow sticking with me through all the ups and downs life brings (aka, delays galore). Kimmie, Michelle, Alisha, Rachel, Erica, Marty, Amber, Missy, Luise, Whitney, Krista, and Savannah — y'all are rock stars.

Big thanks to Grammarly and ProWritingAid for the amazing editing software. If there are any grammatical mistakes, the blame's on me for ignoring a suggested edit. Comma Lovers keep in mind I break rules on purpose and often to create or remove breaks or breaths.

Getting my books visible on platforms like Amazon and into readers' hands is not easy, but my readers and fans keep me going when it sometimes feels too tough to continue. If you want to keep a writer writing and publishing, buy their books and share them with friends.

Onward and upward, my friends!

About the Author

Stephanie Mirro is an Amazon Charts bestselling author and best known for ***The Last Phoenix*** urban fantasy romance series. Stephanie's lifetime love of ancient mythology led to a college major in the Classics, which wasn't as much fun as writing her own fantastical mythology stories. But that education, combined with an overactive imagination and a love for all things fantasy, resulted in a writing career.

Although born and raised in the Southern Arizona desert, Stephanie now resides in Georgia with her husband, two kids, and two furbabies. This thing called "seasons" is still magical.

Interested in the longer, more entertaining story? Visit stephaniemirro.com/about